EX⊕RCIS
TE

VOLUME 1
MARACAS BAY DARK RIVER

First Edition February 2023

Front cover design by Neel Latchman

Editing/Proofreading by Kaylee Labban

Very special thanks to my Beta readers

Amber Goodrich and

Nicolette 'Moons' Joseph

ISBN 979-8-3704-0341-5 (paperback)

CONTENTS

Chapter 1 01

Chapter 2 07

Chapter 3 16

Chapter 4 22

Chapter 5 31

Chapter 6 44

Chapter 7 52

Chapter 8 62

Chapter 9 72

Chapter 10 93

Chapter 11 98

Chapter 12 110

Chapter 13 121

Chapter 14 129

Chapter 15 141

Chapter 16 150

Chapter 17 163

Chapter 18 172

Chapter 19 186

Chapter 20 197

Chapter 21 208

Chapter 22 230

CHAPTER

1

Alister and James returned home after a tragic loss in the Alpines, their family shaken and speechless for days. Losing a father figure and two kids on the night of Christmas eve and one other kid in a coma, the boys returned home conquered by loss. Ravi brought Adelheid back from Switzerland to attend his stepfather's funeral. Ravi had grown distant from Alister and James; he could not bring himself to speak to them since the incident.

EXORCIZAMUS TE

The October family gathered for the funerals of Raphael, Benji, and Shay. It was a gloomy day for the October family, suffering the loss of Raphael and the entire next generation in one fell swoop. Raphael was like a father to all the kids. Acknowledging his tragic end was particularly arduous for Alister, James, and Ravi. Raphael's last wishes were that he be cremated, and instructions for his cremation process were carried out by Ravi.

Ravi wiped the tears from his eyes and placed his hand on Raphael's cold body, "I'm sorry I failed you; there was nothing I could do to save you or the kids. I never want to feel that way again; I don't want to lose anyone again, not like this. Maybe if it were me out there with you, this wouldn't have been the outcome...." Ravi looked up at Alister before continuing. "But the past can't be changed now. I know you were only trying to protect me from this life; I feel responsible, like it's partly my fault. You wouldn't have needed to protect me if I was stronger, and I could have been there with you. Then, maybe a different outcome would have come to pass. Watch over me, dad." Ravi's tears flowed onto Raphael's lifeless body.

Alister and James walked over, each placing their hand on his shoulder without saying a word. Ravi reached into his pocket and retrieved Raphael's lighter. Quickly whispering something in Latin, Ravi ignited the flame and tossed the lighter onto Raphael's body, igniting the fire. The three stood and watched the body burn; Adelheid approached Ravi and held his hand.

"You going to be okay?" Alister asked Ravi.

"That thing is still out there; I will never be okay," Ravi stated. Glaring at Alister, he held his gaze for a moment before slowly turning and walking off with Adelheid in tow.

"I'm sorry—" Alister expressed sadly.

Hearing this, Ravi paused to reply, "Sorry doesn't bring them back or avenge him;

what I am about to do will fix both problems."

Alister and James exchanged looks swiftly. "Ravi, wait, you don't have to do this by yourself," Alister said.

"I know, but I choose to do it alone. I got dad's voicemail too. He sent it to all his contacts; I know he picked you as his legacy. I can live with that, and I wish you the best. But if we do this together, who else stands to die because of your mistakes? I refuse to lose anyone else, nor will I stand by and watch you get anyone else killed," Ravi nonchalantly answered.

Alister took a step back and bowed his head in shame. "He tried his best out there, Ravi; ease up off him with the guilt-tripping," James defended.

"Take a look around you. Do you hear any kids crying for my dad? This, right here, is his best; I don't want to find out what his worst is like. You are family, and I love you guys, both of you, but I lost everything that night; all

I have now is you two and Heidi. I won't watch you fail again; I'm sorry, guys, but I will finish this myself," Ravi responded.

"Call us if you need anything, money, help, information; I've got your back, alright," Alister remarked.

Ravi turned around, approached Alister and James, and hugged them. "Take care of yourselves," he told them.

"Where are you headed now?" James inquired.

"I've got to deal with some legal issues for my dad," Ravi replied.

"Be safe, man," said James.

While slowly walking away, Ravi turned around one last time. "Oh, by the way, the library dad spoke about is not in his office back home. It's in his great grandfather's house, back in Trinidad, a little village called Endeavor; ask for Brij," Ravi advised as he turned and waved at them before leaving.

Alister and James turned to each other.

"Trinidad, huh? I haven't been back there since we left in nineteen ninety-eight; I was, what, four years old? That was twenty-four years ago; you were a newborn back then; you barely lived there," Alister exclaimed.

"Well, what do you say? Trip to the Caribbean?" asked James.

"Home sweet home," Alister declared and bumped fists with James.

CHAPTER

2

At the end of the funeral, Alister and James stayed a few days with their grieving family. They took on as much of the burden as possible to allow their family to be as comfortable as they could be in this harrowing time. Ravi and Adelheid were gone before the funeral ended; no one had seen them since then, and Ravi was not answering calls or replying to messages. After a week of consoling the family, Alister and James hopped on a plane and flew to the twin islands of Trinidad and Tobago.

Stepping off at the Piarco International Airport, Alister and James hopped into a taxi. They chartered it to take them to Endeavor. A lot had changed since Alister was last on the island. They took in the new sites as they journeyed to their destination.

Soon enough, they arrived in Endeavor. What was once a quiet village had become a significant point of interest; clubs, malls, restaurants, and bars lined the streets. At night, the village came alive. Raphael's great-grandfather's house was deep into the rural area of the village. It was a long private stretch of land surrounded by tall grass stretching half a mile inside, sitting on sixteen-hundred acres of land wrapped in an iron fence all the way around.

"Aite fellas, I cyah go too far inside dey. You go have to take it by the gate here," the driver informed them.

"No problem, drive," Alister replied. He paid the driver while James got out and retrieved their bags from the trunk.

The driver honked twice and drove off. Alister and James turned to the massive iron gate before them. Alister took out his phone and looked through the text messages Ravi had sent him on the day of the funeral. Listed there was the number of the groundskeeper, Brij, whom he then dialed.

"Yeah?" a raspy voice answered.

"Hey, is this Brij?" asked Alister.

"Who want to know?" Brij snarked.

"Raphael sent me here. We are his nephews, Alister and James," Alister replied.

"October?" asked Brij after a brief pause.

"That's right," Alister responded.

At the side of the gate was a box with two lights on it, red and green. The green light lit up, and the loud clank of the gate unlocking startled the boys. "How did he know we were outside?" Alister whispered to James, covering the phone.

James looked around; atop the ten-foot gate was a camera. James nudged Alister and pointed to it. "I guess he can see us," James answered.

The call ended without warning. Alister looked at his phone, confused, and placed it back in his pocket. "Alright, guess we have to walk the rest," he told James. They both picked up their bags and entered the gates; the locks slammed shut after they walked in. The boys followed the black gravel road to the house. Looking around, they saw nothing but grass as tall as themselves and could only hear the sound of the fine gravel crunching under their feet.

"I'm worried about Ravi," James suddenly exclaimed.

"Me too, bro. I wish he was here with us, but I can't say that I blame him," Alister replied.

"Don't do that," James chided.

"Do what?" asked Alister.

"Blame yourself for what happened," James responded.

"Ravi had a point. That was me at my best, and I messed up badly—" Alister admitted.

"Uncle Raph was also there; he missed his shot just like you did. You were worried about us, and he was worried about you. Plus, who knows how long he has been after this thing! How can you blame yourself? He died trying to protect us; no one mistake caused all of this. Give yourself a break from the guilt you are carrying for this," James argued.

"You know, I never thought about it like that. I'm so used to burdening myself with everyone's problems that I forgot there are people who did the same for me," Alister replied.

"All we can do now is try and live up to the legacy he left behind; he chose you for a reason. He saw something in you that you don't see in yourself," said James.

"That helps a lot; thanks for that," Alister smiled.

After a grueling half-hour walk in the searing hot tropical sun, Alister and James made it to the door of the two-story house. Sitting on the porch was an old man with short grey hair, glasses, and a plaid shirt. Alister and James tried to compose themselves before speaking to the old man. Alister took a deep breath and stood up straight. "Mr. Brij?" he asked with his hand stretched out.

"You not shame? Young boy like you cyah catch he self yet!" Brij exclaimed.

"It's hot, man," James answered.

"Ize not yuh man, ulyuh just have it too easy. Raphael got soft in the States. If he was here hunting, he wouldna be so rusty and get heself kill," Brij remarked.

"Careful how the fuck yuh talk about my family, eh," Alister sternly retorted.

Brij smirked, "Still have some Trini in

yuh, I see." Brij got to his feet and walked up to Alister. "Brij Mohan the second," he said as he shook Alister's hand.

"I was wondering about that; Uncle Raph said Brij was his great-grandfather. I figured you looked too spry for someone that old," James commented.

"How old yuh think I is?" asked Brij.

"Late fifties, maybe late sixties, tops," James replied.

"Eighty-two, and I could throw licks on two ah ulyuh, busy busy," Brij corrected.

"Think so?" Alister smirked.

"Fuck around and find out, nah!" Brij responded.

"I refuse to hit a dinosaur," Alister stated.

Brij tucked his elbow and swung at Alister's head, crashing it into the side of his face; Alister stumbled and fell into the wall. James dropped his bags and charged at Brij, swinging a right hook at him. Brij ducked under his quick swing and rammed his shoulder into

James' ribs, causing James to stumble into Alister. Alister caught him, and they stopped to compose themselves. Brij laughed at them both. Alister, already bleeding from his cheeks, wiped the blood with his shirt sleeve, and together with James, they charged at Brij. Alister ran in front of James, thrusting a kick forward. Brij sidestepped effortlessly, but James grabbed and held him down. Alister turned and hesitated before punching. Holding back a little, he connected a blow to Brij's face.

"Steups!" Brij shook his head.

Brij whipped his head backward, connecting with James' head and forcing his grip loose.

"Hit like a man!" Brij snarked before he struck Alister, knocking him unconscious. Alister fell to the floor while James held his face in pain. "Oh God, Raphy, you send these boys to dead," Brij mumbled. "Aye, pick up yuh cousin and bring him inside; I go make some tea for ulyuh, come," Brij exclaimed as he opened the front door and motioned James to come inside with his finger.

CHAPTER

3

Alister lay unconscious on the chair; Brij entered the living room with a cup of tea for the boys and an icepack for James. "Yuh go live, doh worry," Brij chuckled.

"For an old man, you're really strong," James commented, holding the icepack to his head.

"In this life, yuh have to be. One moment of weakness and crapaud smoke yuh pipe," Brij remarked.

"What does that mean?" asked James.

"It means yuh fucked," Brij replied.

"Oh," James exclaimed.

"Take a look at yuh cousin; yuh know why he out cold right now?" Brij questioned.

"Because he underestimated how strong you were? He dropped his guard because you were an old man, I guess?" James responded.

"Nah, when yuh had me, two against one, yuh boy hold back he punch. Instead of hitting me as hard as he could, he chose not to. That is the kind of shit that does get yuh killed; hesitate for a moment, and yuh dead. If this was a hunt, that was the end of ulyuh," Brij explained.

"But what if he didn't hold back and it messed you up," asked James.

"Yuh too concerned with what could have happened but not focusing on what is happening. Yuh too soft, both ah ulyuh; there is no place for second thoughts. Yuh have to be ruthless. Act first, think later. Act aside from emotions; if any of those feelings get in the way, yuh go be dead in the blink of an eye. I doh know why Raphael send ulyuh here, but yuh not ready for this life. When yuh boy wakes up, get yuh shit and leave," Brij exclaimed.

"But Raphael—" James was cut off.

"Listen, doh make meh talk twice. Pack yuh shit and get off my property," Brij grunted.

"Now, wait a minute. Uncle Raph said he entrusted this to us," James stated.

Brij drew a revolver from inside his shirt and held it to James' head. "Yuh want me to entrust this bullet to yuh head? Listen to meh, boy, ulyuh not ready for this, and yuh have nothing here. Go back to wherever yuh come from 'cause this isn't for ulyuh. I doh care what Raphael tell yuh. I telling yuh doh come back here," Brij retorted as he pulled the hammer back with his thumb. "Talk back to meh again, and yuh go join Raphael in the afterlife!"

James didn't flinch. With piercing eyes, he stared at Brij, unphased.

"Play mad," said Brij. James held his ground, keeping his gaze on him. Brij took the gun off him and holstered it back into his shirt; he stood up and walked to the window. *They doh belong in this life, but that's the eyes of a hunter. I can imagine what these boys went through to have this kinda conviction. Raphael, I hope yuh know what yuh doing*, Brij thought. "When he wakes up, there is a doctor not far from here; take him there, and tell him I sent you. He will patch yuh up and give yuh things for the pain," Brij finally stated.

James nodded 'yes' and turned to Alister, still out cold on the sofa next to him.

"I have some things to do, but I not leaving ulyuh here alone. Somebody go come while I gone. Doh touch anything till I come back," said Brij. He took his keys off the hook on the wall, walked out the door, got into an old truck, and left. James walked to a window and watched as the truck drove off towards the gate.

James returned to the sofa where Alister

lay and placed the ice pack on his head where he was struck. After several minutes had gone by, James began to feel uneasy. He got up and paced around the room. Catching a glimpse of the other rooms, he hesitantly ventured around the house. He circled the downstairs portion of the house a few times and was tempted to venture upstairs, his eyes looking up ever so often while walking past it.

James turned to look at Alister quickly, then glanced out the window to see if anyone was coming in. Curiosity got the better of him, and he swiftly ran up the stairs. James looked around at the top of the stairs, slowly walking around and looking into the open rooms. He constantly peered through the window to ensure Brij had not returned nor the person he said would come.

Soon James came upon a locked door. Unlike the other rooms, this door was secured by a lock. The door itself and the frame were made of pure iron. James touched the door tentatively; rubbing his index finger and thumb together, he felt a grain-like substance on his fingertips. "Salt?" he wondered aloud. James then inspected the lock closely. There seemed to be no keyhole, but there was a divot in the center in the shape of a star.

Suddenly, the sound of a shotgun racking rendered James motionless. "What part of don't touch anything didn't register in that thick skull, boy?" a woman hissed.

CHAPTER

4

"Please, don't shoot," James begged.

"Yuh lucky it's not Brij; you would be responding with two shots in yuh ass," said the woman. James slowly turned around with his hands raised at his shoulders, mere inches from the barrel of the gun held by a woman with velour black dreadlocks crashing on her shoulders. Her eyes were different colors, the left was galaxy blue, and the right was champagne brown. The white highlights of her locks draped down the side of her half-moon cheekbones. At five feet, two inches, she possessed the body of a goddess.

"Put down the gun," James requested.

"Or what?" the woman shot back.

James subtly looked off to her side and saw Alister peering around the corner of the staircase. Alister tried to ambush her, but his first step triggered the woman to turn and fire at him. He crashed to the ground, holding his midsection in pain.

"Alister!" James shouted, quickly putting the woman in a chokehold from behind. Without hesitation, she dropped the gun's barrel to face James' foot and fired. Amid the pain, James released his hold on her. Changing her grip from the trigger to the gun's barrel, she struck James across the face with the butt of the weapon. She then threw him into the wall with a swift kick to his chest. James made a feeble attempt to swing at her. The woman met his attack with one of her own, making James feel like he had gotten hit with a steel bat. In the blink of an eye, she unleashed a flurry of punches at James. Grabbing onto his jacket, she swung him off the wall, jumping while holding her grip. Using his momentum to turn him around, she placed her foot on his chest and leaned to the ground, flipping James over and kicking him over to Alister.

Alister looked over at James when he heard him fall beside him; moments later, the warm barrel of the gun was pressed against his cheek. The woman pulled the trigger, and a loud audible click came from the weapon.

Alister flinched at the sound, expecting death to come for him. "Boom! And you're dead again in the span of a few seconds. Get up!" she yelled. James and Alister struggled to their feet. With pain radiating through their bodies, they stumbled to reach their feet. The woman took out a walkie-talkie and pressed the side button. "Brij," the woman called out.

"How did they do, Rayna?" asked Brij over the device.

"Barely lasted ten seconds; yuh could come back now," Rayna responded. She took her hand off the button and hooked the walkie-talkie back on her belt. "Downstairs, now!" she ordered while pointing her gun at them.

Alister and James slowly crept down the stairs in pain, Rayna trailing behind them as they took baby steps. Alister and James walked back to the sofa and sat down; Rayna opened a drawer in the next room, took out an orange cylindrical bottle, and tossed it over to them. "Take two for the pain; it will help," she informed them while reaching into the refrigerator and retrieving two bottles of water.

The sound of Brij's truck pulling up to the house was heard before its creaky old door slammed shut, and his heavy footsteps quickly approached; he entered the front door. "We have a saying here: 'Who doh hear, go feel!' Alister, I sure you familiar with it," Brij grunted.

Rayna walked into the room and handed them the bottles of water to take the painkillers she had given them. "It means when you don't listen to advice, you suffer the consequences," Rayna explained, sitting down next to them on the sofa.

Brij walked over and sat on the coffee table across from them. "Look, I think ulyuh is good boys; decent young men. I didn't forget how Raphael talk about ulyuh, but this life is not for good people. Good people are weak; they have a conscience that won't let them do this job effectively. Yuh need to act first and worry about it after. Two ah ulyuh lucky the gun was loaded with salt rounds, but in this life, yuh doh get lucky. Everything out to kill. They not gonna hesitate and think twice. Yuh will die out there, and I sorry, but I not sending no children to die. I doh care what Raphael say, yuh understand?" Brij declared.

"Then teach us," Alister exclaimed.

"This is not a school, and we doh train outsiders. This is a family legacy; Raphael had no business sending just anybody here. He was barely a hunter heself. Raphael was good with research; end of story! He died hunting Krampus out of some petty vendetta. His emotions got in the way, and that is why he not here today. As harsh as that sounds, that is the reality of this life; he should have stayed inside his library where he belong," Rayna answered.

"How can you talk about my uncle like that!" James remarked.

"He was my uncle too, so drop yuh tone with me before I give you something them pills can't ease," Rayna retorted.

"Rayna is only twenty-two, and she almost killed two ah ulyuh without breaking ah sweat. She is still a baby. The two ah ulyuh, doh mind yuh big so, ulyuh is still only children. We doh hunt here; we is only the information center for hunters in the family. So, let that sink in for a lil bit," said Brij.

"In other words, we are the nerds in this family. We are not the fighters, and neither was Uncle Raph. If it was a hunter here instead of me when Brij left ulyuh alone, no doubt yuh was dead," Rayna revealed.

"So, we were never alone? This whole thing was a setup? For what?" asked James.

"To see what yuh woulda do. Following orders is what yuh shoulda do in the first place. Yuh disobey my order, yuh didn't wait for backup, and yuh went anyway and woulda get killed. It have no room for people who doh listen; is people like ulyuh who will get killed and get other people killed in the process," Brij explained.

Alister bowed his head in shame; James' eyes quickly glanced over to him.

"Ahh, I see; it already get somebody kill. So, you responsible for Raphael's death, then? Like yuh try to play hero and realize this is not a movie? Let me at least ease some of the pain for yuh; Raphael knew he was in over he head.

Krampus roamed the earth for centuries; one man was never going to kill it. Maybe if the actual hunters had gone, it might have been a different story," said Brij.

"But instead, Raphael dropped everything and ran off on his own out of revenge, and he caused those kids to die. He was responsible for you and didn't do he job," Rayna continued.

"Doh beat up yuhself. That is not a burden for children," said Brij. "You more than welcome to stay here for a few days. Yuh went through all the trouble to come here, and yuh thought yuh was doing the right thing. Yuh earn some respect for that, but this life is not for you. Rayna will show you to a room; stay as long as you need to and be on your way when yuh ready. It have a lot to see in Trinidad since you leave, Alister; go make the most of it. Yuh go need somebody to let you in and out of this house while yuh here, so Rayna go tag along while yuh here. Just make sure yuh feed she, and she wouldn't beat yuh ass again," Brij suggested with a smile.

"Come, yuh room would be upstairs next to mine," Rayna stated. Alister and James got off the sofa, picked up their bags, and followed Rayna to their room.

CHAPTER 5

Rayna led them to the room closest to the staircase and opened the door. Inside was a cozy room with two beds, an entertainment set-up, a computer, a desk, and a private bathroom. "Wow, this is nicer than our house at home," Alister mumbled.

"This house was an abandoned nursing home back in the days of Brij's father. Brij senior, as we called him, worked a case here back in his days. This was a geriatric nursing home; the place was abandoned after a string of deaths occurred over the years. It went from a few deaths per year to a couple every week. Then rumors began to spread about this place being haunted. Moreover, the patients began committing suicide after going insane and babbling on about seeing a Jumbie," Rayna explained.

"Jumbie? That's the Trini word for ghost, right? If I remember correctly, that is," James remarked, looking over to Alister for confirmation.

"Close. Of course, that is what people call it today, but Jumbie is a different class of evil spirits. Ghosts are the lowest; they can't physically interact with the world, but in cases involving violent deaths or vengeful spirits, they can somewhat interact with the world. Then it has the highest class of ghosts that could possess people," Rayna explained.

Alister and James set down their bags in the room and continued talking to Rayna. "How could they do that but not the others?" Alister enquired.

"Well, people can die in some unholy ways, such as suicide, rape, murder, and violent deaths. That kind of thing breeds evil. Unfortunately, that kind of evil does dutty the souls of the people who passed, and they can't move on to the afterlife or whatever lies ahead. Instead, they remain with all that evil, and over time, it grows, feeding off more and more evil until it is strong enough to possess somebody and make them kill theyself," Rayna answered.

"Why kill themselves? Wouldn't they want revenge or something?" asked Alister.

"Actually, no. They burdened with that evil, and that evil eats away at yuh. After some time, they just want to move on, so they possess people with clean souls and then take their life so they could hitch a ride to the other side and out of limbo," Rayna replied.

"Limbo?" James repeated.

"They neither living nor dead. They can't leave the land of the living, and they can't go

33

back either; they're stuck in the middle of life and death," Alister explained.

"Hmmm, somebody knows dey thing," Rayna stated.

"I did some reading on it since Uncle Raph passed away. Bits and pieces of it, I kinda know," Alister remarked.

"Anyways, yeah. Ghosts possess people to get out of limbo and pass on," Rayna repeated.

"So, how would you stop it? Can you even kill a ghost?" James queried.

Rayna looked at James. "You don't need to know that. Didn't we tell you this life isn't for you?" she snarked.

"Come on, Rayna. Not like we can just go find ghosts anywhere and hunt them, right? What bad could it do to know? Maybe this information might save us; what if we run into a ghost back home one day? That kind of knowledge would be pretty useful, don't you think?" asked Alister.

"I look dotish to you?" Rayna replied.

"No," Alister immediately replied.

"I not gonna be the reason the two ah ulyuh play hero and fight ghosts. No! Leave it alone; dais why we have hunters," Rayna exclaimed.

Alister smiled and sat down on the bed, interlocking his fingers. Leaning forward, he looked up at Rayna. "Fine, if that will help you sleep at night. Because one day, we might run into something we don't know how to deal with, and knowing simple little things like what repels a ghost or what stops it would have saved us and many others. You say Uncle Raphael got those kids killed; I see it as saving four others. Those four can save more and more people over their lifetime; he didn't just save us but indirectly saved everyone we would end up saving or helping. All the good we do is an extension of him because he leveled with us when Krampus came. We didn't know any better before and could have all died. Which side of the future do you want to be on? The side that indirectly helped many people or the side that denied two people information that got them killed later on?" asked Alister.

James smirked. Rayna walked up to Alister, looked at him, and smiled. Alister innocently smiled back at her. Rayna swiftly slapped him across his face, and he uttered a high-pitched squeal upon impact. "Riiiight, you two are going to save people," Rayna chuckled, turned around, walked to the wall, and plugged in a nightlight on the wall outlet. "Just in case ulyuh get scared in the night, plus this will keep away mosquitos, too," she stated before she turned and walked out the door. Alister rubbed his reddened face keeping his eyes on her; James laughed at him for being hit by Rayna.

"You ok?" James giggled.

"Oh, shut up," Alister chuckled.

Alister took out his phone and began typing away.

A couple minutes later, Brij came to the door. "Yuh like the place?" he asked.

"Yeah, this is nice," James replied.

"Good, I have a question for ulyuh. Raphael had a charm on him, lil keychain-looking thing, can't miss it. It had a big star as the main piece," Brij informed them.

"I remember seeing him with it back home. Yeah, I guess; what about it?" Alister enquired.

"Yuh have it?" asked Brij.

"No, why would we have it?" James queried.

"So ulyuh didn't take it off of him for the funeral self before yuh burn the body?" Brij inquired.

"No, we didn't touch the body. The only person close enough to touch the body was Ravi, but we were there. We didn't see him take anything. Why? Is it that important?" asked Alister curiously.

"Me'en telling you. If it burn with him is fine, but if somebody take it, that is a problem," Brij responded.

"You know it would help if you just told us what's so special about it? Ent is just protection against evil?" Alister enquired.

"It has a star on it, right? By chance, it was a star inside a circle?" questioned James.

"Yeah, why?" Brij asked.

"Just trying to figure out if it's the same keychain he always carried or if it was one I didn't know about," James replied.

Brij squinted; he quickly stepped inside the room and walked up to James. "Eh heh, and I must be look like I born yesterday?" Brij exclaimed.

"N… No?" James shook.

"Yuh lying to meh boy? I could smell bullshit from a mile away. Talk now, or I go blaze yuh ass with licks till yuh talk," Brij declared.

"The lock on the room at the other end of the hallway had a divot in it. It looked like a star-shaped object could fit the divot and fill it. I just thought maybe it was a key for that room," James answered.

Brij chuckled, "Ahh boy, yuh put that together fast. I shouldna say nothing; I never thought you woulda make that connection. I didn't even know yuh pay attention to the lock. Yeah, well, since yuh figure it out, is ah key that does open Raphael's library. Everything we know about every evil creature inside them books. It's four generations of knowledge acquired over the years, so yuh could see why I wouldn't want that key just out and about," Brij stated.

"I understand," James answered.

Alister looked at James and Brij; James traded looks with him for a moment. Brij walked back to the door but not before saying, "Do me a favor. Find out if Ravi took the key. I doh want to leave this up to chance; call Ravi and make sure. Let me know when you get him, aite? It getting lil late; ulyuh wah some food? We could order something or ulyuh could take the truck and buy food for we, aite? Fix up," said Brij as he walked off.

"Fuck, that was scary; how the ass he know I was lying about that?" asked James.

"Notice I didn't say anything," said Alister.

James looked at him, confused, "What do you mean? You didn't know about the lock; you had nothing to hide."

"True," Alister replied as he reached into his bag and pulled out Raphael's charm: two mini mason jars of salt and holy water, an iron sword, and a wooden stake, all tethered to a star amulet at the center of it. "But he might have figured out I had this," Alister smirked.

James rushed outside and looked around to see if the hallway was empty. Quietly closing the door, he ran to the bed beside Alister.

"Where did you get this?" James whispered quietly, taking the key chain from Alister.

"I nabbed it off Uncle Raph the night he died. I didn't tell anyone about it. I actually wasn't going to let anyone know I had this, but now that we know it's a key to his library, we can sneak in," Alister replied.

"And do what? You want Brij to shoot us for real? Those salt rounds hurt, you know. I don't want to imagine what real bullets feel like," James whispered.

"We not gonna get caught; we just need to wait until it's empty here. We'll go in, take pictures of the books we find, and be on our way. How long would that take? An hour? Maybe two or three? We could do that while they sleep, no problem," Alister suggested.

"Are you insane? You know how long it could take to snap pictures of every page?" asked James.

"Then we can take a video and flip through quickly; we can pause at each page and get the snapshots after. Easy work!" Alister advised.

"I think this is a bad idea," James replied.

"He left this to us. They owe us this; I just want what is rightfully ours now. I'm doing this because Uncle Raphael trusted me with it," Alister exclaimed.

***

Brij and Rayna sat on the sofa downstairs, watching the live footage of James and Alister, streamed by a hidden-away camera disguised as a nightlight/mosquito repellent pod across from them. "Wah I tell yuh? I know these two jackasses had it," Brij stated.

"Them feel they smarter than everybody," Rayna replied with a smirk. "Why yuh think Uncle Raphael pick them?"

Brij stayed silent for a moment, "I think I have an idea. James, the one with the muscles, he have ah intensity about him. Gun to he head, and the man didn't even blink. He's the same one who figured out Raphael's keychain was a key for the upstairs library. He have some potential, but I doh know what that next jackass doing here," said Brij

"I doh know, nah," Rayna stated.

"Keep ah eye on them, and keep them outta trouble while they here," Brij told her, patting her head.

CHAPTER
6

Alister and James got settled in. Nightfall came quickly in Endeavor. Alister used the laptop in the room and did some research while James lay in bed, texting the family to see how everyone was doing at home. Brij made a pot of tea and sat outside on the porch with his cup while smoking a cigar. Rayna showered and changed, stepped out of her room, and knocked on the door of Alister and James.

She gently pushed the door open and peeked her head inside. "Lewe go for some food; we go take a lil drive," she smiled and told them before retracting her head from the room. Alister and James looked at each other, got up, and headed downstairs. "Ulyuh have money?" asked Brij from outside.

"We have a card; we're ok," Alister answered.

"Good, lewe go. I driving," said Rayna, grabbing their hands and yanking them outside with her. Coming through the door, Brij tossed the keys to the truck; without looking, Rayna raised her hand and caught it. The trio entered the truck and left; Brij waved at them as they drove off.

Brij took out his phone and replayed a voicemail again, the same one that was sent to Alister the night Raphael died. "I cyah shake this feeling, Raphael; why the ass you choose Alister as your legacy and not Ravi. I know yuh too good, yuh wouldn't make a decision like that unless yuh know yuh was gonna do something dotish and get yuhself killed. That boy is not hunter material; I wish yuh had tell meh why yuh pick he," Brij mumbled to himself as he sipped his tea.

***

Rayna and the boys pulled up to the food strip near a mall. The trio got out and inhaled the incredible aroma of the Caribbean dishes on the strip, so succulent they could almost taste it. This was a familiar scent to the boys; it smelled like home whenever they had family get-togethers. As a child, Alister had grown up in this little village, and this same food strip was also where his family had met Raphael, he recalled. They each got something to eat and bought extra for Brij. After getting their food, they returned to the truck and drove around the village. Rayna showed Alister and James what was new since they had left the island. Soca music filled the streets as they drove passed the bars on the main road.

The three bobbed their heads to the music. Rayna danced while driving, and Alister, holding her food, fed her bites as she drove while also eating his own food. This was all too familiar to the boys; they grew up in this culture so they felt at ease. James wasn't as exposed to this; he was only a baby when they had left Trinidad, so he grew to adapt to his new environment. Alister could switch between the two depending on who he spoke with. Rayna took them out of the village and drove them around.

"Where we headed?" asked Alister.

"Maracas," Rayna responded.

"The beach? Now?" Alister enquired.

"Yuh never go beach in the night?" asked Rayna with a smile.

"Not really," Alister replied.

"What about Brij? His food is still here; shouldn't we drop it off for him before we leave?" James wondered aloud.

"Awww, yuh too sweet. Nah, doh worry about Brij. Once he have he tea, he ok. He really just wanted us to get food. Whenever we go back, he will eat. One thing that man not fussy about is food," Rayna explained.

"Why Maracas, though? That's kinda far; we would take over ah hour to reach," questioned Alister.

"Yuh know yuh doh have to talk Trini for me. I could understand yuh just fine. Just be yuhself, is cool," said Rayna with a smile.

"Trini to the bone. Some things yuh cyah grow out of," Alister returned her smile.

"So how come you does talk so, but James doh have the accent and dialect," Rayna enquired.

"Well, I learned to speak in America, so for me, it was what I grew up hearing. Even though they talk like you at home, I grew accustomed to speaking without the Trinidadian accent for school while talking to friends and stuff, so it stuck. But I understand the dialect just fine, like when you say 'yuh,' you mean 'you,' 'dais' means 'that is,' and 'ulyuh' means all of you. I get that, but what I have trouble with is Trini sayings like 'crapaud smoke yuh pipe.' Things like that."

"So the girls away doh like the Trini accent?" asked Rayna curiously.

"They love it; they like it when Alister is around. My friends make him talk a lot just to hear his accent, but only if they ask him to do it. Normally, he would speak without it," James answered.

"How it does be in America? I never leave Trinidad; Brij would never let me go," Rayna enquired.

"Brij is your great-grandfather, right? Was Uncle Raph also your uncle?" asked James.

"You're asking 'cause I'm black, and my last name is Mohan?" Rayna chuckled. "Dad is East Indian, and mom is Afro-Trinidadian. I took more to her side. Don't worry; it does trip up rel people. They see the name, but they look twice when they see the dreadlocks. I could say the same about you; Alister October doesn't sound Trini or East Indian, so nobody would really expect to see an Indian."

"Well, like you, I take after my mom. She is East Indian, while my dad is American. They met while he vacationed here with his family. He ended up staying for her, and, well after I was born and they got married. Dad moved us up to the States with his family. Uncle Raph married mom's sister, so he also left Trinidad to come and live there with us," Alister replied.

"So, what about Ravi? Why is he not here?" asked Rayna. "I grew up with Ravi when I was younger; Raphael took him everywhere he went."

"Ravi isn't on speaking terms with us right now; he took his stepdad's death really hard. Of course, he was more like a father to Ravi than his actual father. He never referred to Uncle Raph as his stepdad; to him, that was his dad. He was basically a father figure to all of us," Alister answered.

"I see," said Rayna. The trio continued eating for the rest of the ride, now just a few minutes from the beach.

CHAPTER

7

They arrived at the beach a little after nine o'clock. The moonlight illuminated the sand on the shores and sparkled off the water's surface. Rayna parked on the sand; they got out, took off their shoes, and walked along the shoreline with their toes in the sand. "It's been so long since I've seen this place; I used to visit with my parents for the holidays. Mom has a friend who lives in the village we just passed. I remember waking up at five in the morning and coming to the beach to play in the freezing cold water. I always did favor colder temperatures," said Alister.

"Oh, are you talking about Aunty Asha?" James asked.

"Yeah, that's her. Man, I haven't seen her in over twenty years; she may not recognize me," Alister mused. "I remember falling and busting my chin one time; blood was squirting out, and she ran home with me in her hands."

"Yuh know, we could pass and check them before heading home if yuh want. The village is walking distance," Rayna exclaimed.

"Really? That would be great; I'd love to see how she and Curtis are doing. I'll get some pics with them; mom would be so surprised," Alister replied.

"Cool, then we go pass on we way back," Rayna agreed. "Also, when yuh take a swim? How yuh so wet?"

Alister looked at Rayna, confused. "What—" Alister uttered before being pushed by her. Rayna placed her foot across the front of Alister's before pushing him so he fell into the tiny waves crashing on the shore, making a splash. James and Rayna fell on the sand laughing at how he had fallen. Alister quickly got up and tried to dust himself off and dry off the water.

"Nah!" Alister shouted. Alister ran to Rayna and reached his hand out to grab her off the ground. While laughing, Rayna rolled back and sprung to her feet, jumping away and narrowly escaping Alister's hand. She reached out, grabbed his hand, and pulled him forward. Losing his balance from overreaching, he fell again into the sand.

"Cyah catch me so easy," Rayna chuckled.

"You alright, Alister?" James laughed, still lying on the sand.

Alister looked up at Rayna and pushed off the ground; steadily, he got to his feet and dusted off the sand clinging to his clothes.

"Ulyuh wanna play a game?" asked Rayna.

"What game?" James replied.

"Well, last person standing wins," Rayna responded with a grin.

"And what do we get if we win?" Alister enquired.

"The joy of winning? I doh know?" Rayna replied, chuckling.

"Let's make it interesting. If we win, you give us access to Raphael's library for one hour," Alister informed her.

Rayna's playful demeanor instantly changed. "Nah, no fucking way," she answered.

"Scared?" Alister teased.

"No! this just doh benefit me. What I getting out of this?" Rayna shot back.

"Name your price," Alister replied.

"Oh, yuh think money important?" Rayna quipped.

"You must want something bad enough to wager unless you are not sure of yourself?" Alister commented.

"Just forget it," said Rayna.

"So, there is something?" Alister provoked.

"I said forget it!" Rayna barked.

"You know, you play like you're this hard girl, but you might be the biggest coward I know. You always follow orders like a good little soldier?" Alister retorted.

"Watch yuhself—" Rayna snapped.

"Think for yourself for once, or do you need Brij's permission to do that, too?" asked Alister.

"Yuh know, I could just leave yuh here with yuh dotish self," Rayna responded.

"You would still be Brij's little puppet, but go ahead; it might be the closest you come to making a real decision for yourself," Alister goaded.

Rayna walked up to him, clenching her jaw. Looking up at the six-foot-two Alister, she muttered, "Fine, yuh want a wager! If yuh win, yuh get yuh hour in the library. If I win, I get to shoot yuh, and not with salt rounds this time!"

"Alister, no!" James exclaimed.

"Deal!" Alister immediately agreed.

"Bet! What are the terms of the wager?" asked Rayna.

"Touch the water, you lose. Last person dry wins," Alister explained.

"Done, I accept!" said Rayna.

"Good, GO!—" Alister threw himself back as soon as their wager began. He fell into the water at the shoreline, a broad smile plastered across his face.

Rayna was baffled and stunned momentarily as she watched Alister on the ground, the water crashing over him. She walked over to him and looked down. "What the fuck yuh doing? You know yuh just lost, right?" said Rayna as the waves crashed over her feet.

"I know; who said I wanted to win?" Alister exhaled profoundly and smiled gently at her.

"Yuh remember if you lose, yuh get shoot, right?" Rayna questioned.

"It was worth it. I mean, you made a call all on your own. Not to judge you, but I see how you are with Brij, and how you hang around him like a lost puppy. It broke my heart when you said Brij would not let you leave the country. It's not what Raphael taught us; he always protected the kids and tried to keep us out of this hunter life, but Brij molded you into it. I can't imagine what that must have done to you; the toll was heavy when things came to light for us, so I can't imagine it being any better for you. I just wanted you to see that you could make your own decisions and not let anyone else hold you back. There is a whole world out there not filled with monsters," Alister exclaimed.

"And yet, you came here to be a part of the world where monsters hide," Rayna remarked.

"I lost all my nieces and nephew in one night, and Raphael died protecting us. I owe it to them to do something, and I feel responsible for it. I took them on that trip but wasn't strong enough to keep them safe. And when it mattered, I slipped up, and it cost the lives of three people in one go. This legacy he left for me is all that's keeping me going. I don't know what I'll do if I can't even do this for him… For them—" Alister explained.

"And yuh choose to lose a wager in which yuh take a bullet from a shotgun?" asked Rayna, baffled.

Alister chuckled. "No, I choose to distract you enough to make you forget that James is also a part of this wager. Your game included him, too," Alister replied. He smiled and winked at her, pointing at the water crashing over her feet.

"Yuh lil—" Rayna snapped, looking down at the water touching her feet. *Touch the water, you lose; last person dry wins;* she recalled his words then.

"You were too busy focusing on me trying to rile you up. I sure you probably see through that; you know I was trying to get a rise out of you, but you kept your calm and accepted the wager, knowing your emotions weren't in the way. But you were so focused on me that you forgot one little detail," said Alister.

Rayna smiled and reached her hand out to pick Alister up and off the ground. Alister grabbed her hand, and she pulled him up. When she let go halfway, he stumbled and fell back into the water. James and Rayna laughed at him as he came out of the water soaking wet.

"Yuh not getting in my truck like that. Yuh could lay down in the tray on the way back, just doh let police see yuh and we good," Rayna exclaimed.

"That sounds good to me," Alister replied, kicking up water and splashing Rayna, as they laughed at each other.

CHAPTER 8

Alister, James, and Rayna walked along the beach, sharing stories of their childhoods and poking fun at each other. "Hey, guys, it's getting kind of late; I want to go see Aunty Asha before they go to bed. They've got a minimart that closes soon; I could catch them before they do," said Alister.

"Already? We only here a lil while now," Rayna exclaimed.

"Well, here's what, I can run over to the village. It's only like a twenty-minute walk from here. I can meet you guys back here afterward. I just want to pop in and say hi," Alister suggested.

"Sure, that works," James replied.

"Yuh want a drop? We could always pick yuh up after, too; just call," Rayna offered.

"No, it's fine; I'm happy to stretch my legs a bit. Call me if anything changes. See you guys in a bit," Alister answered as he waved, turned around, and jogged off into the distance.

"I kinda hungry; yuh want some food?" Rayna asked James.

"Didn't we just eat?" James enquired.

"Yuh point?" Rayna smirked.

"I'm still feeling a bit full, but we could go get something for you," James replied.

"Good, well, come on then. A lil way up ahead, have the food court and bar. We could get some drinks, and I go get a bake and shark. Cyah come to Maracas and not eat a bake and shark!" Rayna professed. James and Rayna looked back to see Alister jogging toward the street in the distance.

***

Alister jogged along the road they came. The road to the village was at the top of a small hill just before the beach. Making his way to the top, he turned around and saw Rayna and James walking along the sand and coconut trees on the beach under the moonlight. There were two entrances to the little fishing village: the road for vehicles, which was only a few meters ahead, and a little man-made track, built with steps from the hill to the road that led inside the village. Alister remembered going up and down those steps as a child, excited to go to the beach and play in the cold water just before the sun came up on the horizon.

The trail was well-lit by streetlights; Alister took his time going down the steps and made it to the road. From there, it was only a few minutes walk along the road before he got to Asha's minimart. Looking at his watch, the time was nine forty-five; the minimart usually closed at ten because it was set up at their house and mainly used by the villagers. So, their opening hours were more flexible than a regular minimart that would be closed by eight o'clock. With fifteen minutes to spare and the house only ten minutes away, Alister took his time and strolled through the street. He remembered every detail just as it was when he was a kid. His hands were in his pockets as he slowly walked the road alone, looking around at the houses.

A strong aroma of fish and seawater filled the air. It was a pleasant aroma that was nostalgic to him, a smell he could only find in this little fishing village. One thing was different, however. Alister remembered the streets being livelier. Villagers would often sit outside and gather at the roadside to chat; they were some of the most welcoming and friendly people he had ever met. Even as a child, it was safe for him to go out alone at night and walk those streets without any care in the world. The community was such a safe and joyful place and remained that way twenty-four years later.

***

James and Rayna left the sandy shore and crossed the street barefoot; they walked across an empty parking lot and over to the food court. Rayna found it strange; the food court looked different, and it wasn't normal for the beach to be this quiet. After closer inspection upon entering the gates, she noticed all the stalls were closed. "What?" she mumbled.

"Closed? Damn, I was beginning to feel for one of those bake and sharks you mentioned," James remarked.

"It odd to see the food court closed, even for a random weekday. The bar always pumping, and people always here," Rayna explained, confused. She walked closer to a stall and pointed to the sign hanging on the booth. "This is a night-time food stall; they open late for bar customers. I don't understand why they closed today," she continued.

"Maybe they took a day off?" James mused.

Rayna looked around, slowly turning her head from side to side, her eyes wandering. "Listen...," she whispered.

James stood quiet for a moment. "I don't hear anything," he exclaimed.

"Exactly... There's a bar just across this food court; we should be hearing people and music. It doh be this quiet!" Rayna told him.

"It's not uncommon for a slow day during the week," James stated.

"Not in Trinidad. Just now is Old Years; school out, and this is holiday time. So, people liming every day. This weird to see the place so empty," Rayna informed him. "Come, lewe go by the bar; at least we go get some drinks."

Rayna and James walked through the food court stalls, still looking around, hoping to see one open. They hopped the fence separating the food court from the bar instead of walking all the way around. To Rayna's surprise, they found the bar empty, closed, and in complete darkness.

"Widdi ass is this?" Rayna mumbled.

James landed next to her and looked up at the closed establishment, too. "Closed?" James muttered.

"I coming here for years. I don't ever remember a time when I was on the beach, and this bar was closed at night, at least not before twelve. Usually, this place is open till two in the morning on a busy night, or midnight at the very least," Rayna exclaimed.

"Well, you're the Trini; I'll take your word for it," James stated.

"No public holidays, no curfews by the government, no reason I could think about why this place would be closed during peak liming season," Rayna mumbled.

James looked around and walked toward the street, checking up and down the road to find no other cars or people in sight. "Hey, Rayna, if this place is as busy as you say during the holidays, where are all the people?" James asked.

Rayna also walked to the street and looked around. "Yuh know... Dais a good question. Where everybody if they not in the bar? Normally it would have campers on the beach or maybe a handful of people on the shore, but I don't remember seeing anybody. Not strange, 'cause where we parked, it's usually empty. Dais why I does go that side, it further from the bar. Come, lewe go see if anybody on the beach." Rayna grabbed his hand and pulled him forward, hurrying to the water again.

***

Alister arrived at Asha's house; the minimart had already been closed even though he had arrived before ten. He approached the door and knocked three times. "Goodnight!" he called out in a deeper distorted tone to mask his voice.

"We close! Go from here," Curtis, Asha's husband, shouted.

"Curtis, dais you?" asked Alister in the same voice, smiling and waiting to see the shock on their faces when they found out who was at the door.

"Shop closed, bhai. Come out the road, go home," Curtis called out shakily.

"Aunty Asha, you home?" asked Alister; listening carefully, he could hear mumbling inside.

"Who really outside, bhai?" asked Curtis curiously.

"Peep by the window," said Alister, walking a few steps to the side to be in view of the window. The curtain pulled slightly, and an eye peeped through.

"Who is you? I doh know you!" Asha declared.

"You doh remember me? I buss my chin when I was small, and you pick me up like a baby and run home by my mother," Alister replied with a smile.

The silhouettes of Asha and Curtis could be seen turning to each other quickly and running out of the room. He could hear their heavy footsteps inside the wooden house as they rushed to the door. The locks clicked, and the door swung wide open. "Nah! Yuh lieee! Alister?" asked Asha with a huge smile.

Alister smiled and nodded at her; Asha grew emotional and covered her mouth. Alister took her in his arms, hugging her tight. "So good to see ulyuh," Alister whispered.

"Come, come, come. Come inside," Curtis excitedly invited him in after hugging Alister too.

They quickly went back into the house and closed the door.

CHAPTER 9

Rayna and James returned to the shoreline of Maracas beach; looking around, they saw no one else, not even the locals. "Strange, I never see the beach this empty before. I does usually come up here for dates," said Rayna.

"Is that a bad thing?" asked James.

"No… I doh think it's a bad thing, but it feeling off," Rayna explained as she scratched her head in confusion.

"Well then, let's just take advantage of this. How often can you say you were the only person on the beach!" James exclaimed.

Rayna looked at him and smiled. "I guess yuh right," she answered. "Come, I'll show yuh some of my spots on the beach."

She reached out her hand, and James, looking down at her open palm, placed his hand in hers, their fingers interlocking. Rayna smiled and looked up at him.

***

Alister sat next to Curtis and Asha at the house, sipping bottled water as they spoke. They reminisced about the past when Asha lived next door to Alister's mom, who repeatedly commented about how big Alister had grown from the tiny kid they remembered. Alister asked them to take a picture with him to send to his mom; the three huddled together and took several pictures.

73

"Oh, let's go take a picture with the child," Asha suggested. "Yuh mother go like she."

Curtis and Asha got up and led Alister to the bedroom where a little girl slept on their bed. "She's so cute. Awww, what's her name?" Alister asked, smiling warmly.

"Maleah," Asha answered.

"She's adorable," Alister told Asha.

"She gonna turn six soon. Just now she go be a big sister," said Asha excitedly. She placed her hand on her slightly bulging stomach and moved her palm in a circular motion over it. She looked down at her belly and then at Curtis, who leaned in and kissed her.

"Yuh lie! Oh gosh, mom go love this," Alister exclaimed.

"Yeah, she better bring she tail and come spend some time with we. Know how long me eh see meh girl. Dais meh liming padna, inno," Asha declared.

"I'll bring she. Yuh know how much she like children," Alister stated.

"Well, this one due in about six months, so she go have two to play with when she come," Curtis told him.

"Oh, come, come. Lewe take a pic of Maleah sleeping. Uncle Curtis, you and Aunty Asha point at she belly so mom would know ulyuh expecting a next one soon," Alister suggested.

"Yeah yeah, come, darlin'," Asha said as she pulled Curtis next to the bed. Both of them sat on the edge, and Alister took the picture.

"Perfect," Alister declared.

"Leme see it," Asha said excitedly.

Alister pulled up the picture, and they huddled over each other to see when Alister noticed something in the picture.

***

Rayna and James strolled back to the truck along the shore, walked passed it, and headed down the beach in the opposite direction they initially went when they first arrived. There, a concrete jetty extended one hundred and fifty meters into the ocean. "This is your spot? Wouldn't everyone know where this was? If I was a kid, I would run up and down this thing and look down at the water," James remarked, confused.

"That's exactly what everybody does. At night, it's a little less crowded, but it still have people now and then," Rayna exclaimed as she sat on the edge of the jetty and hung her feet off. She tapped the concrete next to her for James to sit beside her. James carefully sat down next to Rayna. "But this too open to be my spot," she continued. Rayna slid forward and hopped off the edge. James panicked and tried to stop her from falling. She landed on a ledge that extended out a few feet, enough for one to stand comfortably on. Rayna looked up at James and smiled. Ducking down, Rayna walked along the ridge under the jetty and sat in a hollowed-out area big enough to stand upright or lay flat on the ground. "Jump down," she called out to James.

James hesitantly slid off the jetty's edge onto the concrete ledge below. He turned and saw Rayna sitting in the hollowed-out portion under the jetty; he carefully walked over to her and crouched down to keep his balance. A wave gracefully crashed into the jetty and splashed water upwards at them. James flinched and froze up on the ledge, afraid to lose his balance. Rayna reached out her hand and held on to James, gently guiding him to her.

He stepped into the hollowed-out portion of the jetty and sat beside Rayna. "This is my spot; only a few people have ever come here before," Rayna told him.

"I feel honored," James responded jokingly.

A wave crashed into the side of the jetty, and the moonlight glimmered through the water droplets that splashed by the opening they sat in.

"I had my first kiss here. Sixteen years old, and I was here for a weekend, camping. One of the campers had a son who was a year older than me. We came up here on the jetty a night when we couldn't sleep; we walked along the beach for a while and found weself here. Me, being a little adventurist, I jumped down when I saw the ledge and found this hollowed-out section. It started to rain, so me and the guy was sheltering here and talking about school and books and stuff, and I was a big nerd, so I was crushing hard on him. I doh know how, but it slip out meh mouth, and I said, 'Just kiss me already.'

"Before I get to process that I didn't say that in my head, meh boy lean over, and jeez, sweetest lips I ever tasted was that red man. Never see him again. All where I look on social media, it never turn up anything," Rayna reminisced.

"Wow, like something straight out of a romance movie," James teased.

"Shut up, doh laugh at meh story," said Rayna, bumping James with her elbow.

"Sorry," James chuckled.

"What about your first kiss?" asked Rayna.

"Me? I didn't have one," James answered nonchalantly.

"Yuh lie. Serious? Howww?" Rayna asked.

"I don't know, no reason, really. Just never really happened," James answered.

"Bredda yuh is twenty-four; you telling me you never kiss a girl before?" Rayna pried.

"Pretty much; I guess I don't really have or didn't have time between school, studying, and work, you know? Just stayed focused; never really bonded like that," James explained.

"That kinda sad," Rayna exclaimed.

"I don't feel sad. I am happy with the way I am. I didn't feel like I was missing anything, you know? I have good friends, a good job, and

a good family. I felt fulfilled for the most part,"
James told her.

"And you leave all that to come here to
learn about hunting?" Rayna questioned.

"Well, when your family loses the next
generation of kids and the most influential
father figure in one night by an ancient demon
God, or whatever the hell Krampus is, it
changes things," James replied.

"So it's for revenge, then?" Rayna pried.

"No, not exactly. Alister is the closest
family I have; he practically raised me, despite
being only four years older. There is nothing
we wouldn't do for each other, but on the night
Krampus came, he saved us. Before all of this,
all Alister was trying to do was make everyone
happy. He took the family to experience a white
Christmas in a beautiful place. He sent them on
a mini vacation on his dime, but this thing came
to us and destroyed our family. Alister might
not see it this way, but he did save us. Had he
not done the things he did, we would have all

died. He was ready to die for us, sacrifice himself to save those kids and us… I couldn't lose him; as dark as this sounds, I would rather lose those kids than let him kill himself.

"A part of me would have died inside if it was him that night. The only reason I am in one piece right now is that he gives me hope. I know no matter what, he always has my back. Many people can say that, but almost none of them get the chance to prove it, and he did that without hesitation. He chose to carry on Raphael's legacy without a second thought; it's just who he is. He carries the weight of the world on his shoulders; I just want to be there so he doesn't have to bear the burden all by himself because if the roles were reversed, he would do the same for me. There is no doubt in my mind," James explained.

"Raphael willingly took you guys there? Knowing Krampus was loose in the Alps?" Rayna asked, perplexed.

"No, according to Ravi, he was supposed to be on a business trip. Little did we know he was hunting the damn thing. It's because he was tracking it that we ended up there in the first place. Ravi found his files and saw him checking out a house. Seeing that it was for sale, he showed it to Alister because he knew he loved those things. Only this time, Alister had the money to buy it instead of just admiring it," James told her.

Rayna looked at James as another wave crashed and misted the seawater onto their skins. Suddenly, the loud scream of a woman startled James and Rayna; they both flinched at the unexpected sound coming from the distance. Rayna acted quickly. Stepping out on the ledge, she peeked around the jetty in the direction of the scream. The beach and the road remained empty. She peered over the top of the jetty but still couldn't see any signs of a person. "Do you see anything?" James whispered.

"Nothing, the place still empty," Rayna replied.

"Maybe it's someone from the village? I saw houses on this side. Could it be from there?" asked James.

"This side of the beach is another fishing village, well, kinda. This is where they does bring in the fishing boats. It's two parts of the same village, separated on either side of the hill. The main road and river that flows into the sea does cut through it. Come, we getting out of here. Lewe go see what happen," Rayna suggested.

"What? Why?" asked James.

"Doh be a baby. Come, we doh hada intervene; we just wanna maco what going on," Rayna proposed as she hopped back up to the top of the jetty and pulled James up.

The two ran down the jetty, following where they heard the scream, their feet stomping in the sand as they ran toward the village. Rayna reached the street, still as empty as when they got here before. "Look for lights on in any house. Somebody hada be waking," Rayna advised.

"And then what?" James enquired.

"Ent you from a Trini household? Yuh mother them never maco before?" Rayna questioned.

"Yeah, they mind people's business, but from afar, in their own house, or on social media," James answered.

Rayna chuckled, "Well, out here, we does get more nosey. We want to see up close and personal."

James looked around, his eyes seeking a window with the lights on inside. Turning his body to the right, a shadow on the ground caught his eye. Curled on the floor was a homeless man, shaking at the base of a small coconut tree. "Rayna," James nudged her.

Rayna looked over to see the man on the ground. Pulling James behind her, she said,

"Yoo, I know you. Ent yuh does beg for money outside the bar?"

The man trembled and nodded his head 'yes.' "What yuh doing on the village side? Yuh bothering these people?" Rayna asked sternly. "Come, go up the road. Doh harass the villagers, nah man. Go back to the other side of the beach." The man vehemently refused to do so.

James watched on as Rayna continued to speak to the homeless man. "You want food? Come, I'll give you some food and some money, but doh bother the villagers; they go run yuh, man," Rayna stated.

"I not going back on that side," answered the man with a shaken voice.

"Come, come, yuh cyah stay here. Yuh wah them call police?" asked Rayna

"Police cyah help—" the man replied.

James looked at the man, noticing the fear in his eyes. "What does that mean?" James enquired.

"I does see it," the man responded.

"See what?" Rayna asked, her demeanor instantly turning serious.

***

Alister hugged Asha and Curtis and said his goodbyes. They begged him to stay the night, but he assured them he could not. Asha pleaded with him to spend the night and leave in the morning, telling him she didn't want him going out at night alone. He informed them that his friends were with him and that they would pick him up. He also mentioned that he was supposed to meet them back on the beach and that they were probably waiting for him. Curtis peeked outside, looked at Asha, and subtly nodded at her.

"Ok, hurry and go back. Reach safe, ok," said Asha.

"Why do you sound so concerned?" asked Alister curiously.

Curtis and Asha looked at each other. "A couple months now, people started saying all kinda things. People bawling dey see something outside or on the beach, all kinda things, but they see it mostly near the river. Nobody take it serious 'cause is people who come to the beach say they seeing something in the bush by the food court. Then people in the bar say they see something in the back there too. Is only when a few people from this side ah the village started saying the same thing they stop going outside after dark. Some people cyah help it 'cause they does reach home late. But them people who does be walking late in the night say does hear things and see things. The village frightened ever since, so nobody does really chance it; everybody agreed to keep out ah the road if they could until morning," Curtis explained.

"What kinda things?" Alister queried.

"Nobody really see it, see it. They say it's shadows and voices, but dey pores does raise, and they does get a bad feeling," Asha replied.

"Ulyuh ever see anything?" asked Alister.

"Nah, thankfully, we never see anything, but Maleah scream out a night saying she see something," Asha answered.

"That was for Halloween. We was out in the minimart selling, and the road was pack with people. She see one of them children that dress up," said Curtis.

"She say what she see?" asked Alister.

"Nah, she just started bawling out and crying," Curtis responded.

"Child frighten so bad she get sick, yuh know. Bad, bad fever. She does sometimes be sleeping the whole day. Yuh ent see she didn't wake up with all the commotion we making out here?" asked Asha.

"Yeah, I notice that," Alister commented.

"Yeah, for a while now, she feeling weak; she not eating and thing properly. She doh want no food. The child only eating fruits and vegetables. Maleah even say the food we cook does burn she stomach," Curtis mentioned.

"I make all kinda thing, but the child wouldn't stomach it. I make punch, ice cream, and even cake. I does give she snacks, but she only want fruits," Asha told Alister.

"Well, that not so bad; fruits healthy, at least. I hope she feel better and start eating more solid food. Anyways, leme see to go, ok. I don't want to leave them alone for too long on the beach; we hada go back home soon. It was nice seeing ulyuh again; I missed ulyuh soo much. I will tell mom you asked for her, ok?" Alister said before hugging them and hurrying out the door.

From the window, Curtis and Asha watched Alister quickly jog down the street.

***

Rayna and James stooped down to speak to the homeless man. "What yuh does see?" asked Rayna.

***

As Alister jogged along the street quickly, Rayna listened to the homeless man tell her, 'She does come out at night.' Alister approached the river that ran through the village. 'Yuh does hear a child crying in the road,' the man continued. The sound of an infant broke the dead silence and reached Alister's ear. Turning his attention to the direction of the river, mud, and bamboo peeked through the darkness along the riverbank. 'She does come for yuh. I see she drag somebody in the bush, and all yuh does hear is the scream,' the man told Rayna. Alister looked deep into the darkness; the glimmer of the streetlight faintly lit the dark blue fingers stained with blood that grabbed onto a bamboo shoot, the sound of the bamboo and leaves crackling.

***

Rayna stayed focused on the man as he finished his sentence, "That scream... Yuh does bawl, but nobody could hear yuh. They does call it ah—" the man stopped.

"Call it what?" James asked, looking down; the twinkle on the ground averted James' gaze. He saw a pool of blood flowing on the floor. The man's hand dropped from his chest, where he was bleeding heavily. Neither James nor Rayna noticed it because of his dark clothing and how he was hidden from the light under the tree.

Rayna looked at James, and they knew they needed to run. James and Rayna sprinted to the truck without needing to say a word to each other. "Call yuh cousin, James! Tell him doh go outside! We coming for him now!" Rayna ordered while running. Rayna and James got to the truck and hopped in; James dialed Alister's phone while Rayna started the truck. Another scream filled the dismal beach in the direction of the village where Alister ventured.

"Fuck…," Rayna mumbled as she started the truck.

"Pick up, pick up, pick up," James muttered in a panic.

Rayna pulled off in a hurry and drove off the sand to the main road. The truck's tires squealed as she floored the acceleration; the truck drove to the top of the hill but slowed down due to its steep incline. A loud crash in the back of the truck shook the entire vehicle; Rayna and James screamed out and turned around to see what had made that sound. Out popped Alister's hand, knocking the glass fervently and screaming to drive. Rayna drove off hastily and left Maracas with Alister in the truck's tray.

CHAPTER

10

Rayna drove quickly along the mountain; James rolled down the window and stuck his head out, looking back at the tray "Alister! You good man?!" James shouted.

"No! I am not!" Alister yelled back.

"What happened?!" James retorted.

"I saw some banshee screaming mother fucker in the river!!! What the hell do you think!" Alister replied.

Rayna called out to Alister, "Hold on tight; I go get we out ah here! I can't stop for you to come inside the truck now!"

"Why not?" James asked. Looking ahead, James leaned back in his seat quickly. Standing in the middle of the road was a woman dressed in white, with long dark hair flowing over her face, her skin blue and black and rotting. She held what looked like an infant in her arms, covered in blood as it dripped out onto the street and her white dress. Rayna floored the acceleration keeping a tight grip on the steering wheel.

"Come through, yuh bitch," Rayna mumbled, driving the truck straight into the woman. She disappeared into smoke on impact, letting out a high-pitched screech. Alister was frantic in the tray; hearing the cry again, he panicked.

"Guys! What the fuck was that?!" he yelled as he grabbed hold of the side of the tray. That's when he noticed a reddish-black bruise on his forearm in the shape of a handprint. "What's this?" he mumbled. Having a flashback to a few minutes ago when he saw the entity in the river, he remembered it calling out to him for help while holding the child in hand. Alister had then looked around to see if anyone else was nearby to assist this person who seemed battered and bloody. The moment he took his eye off the woman, she disappeared, and suddenly, she was beside him, grabbing his arm and screaming in his ear.

"What the hell was that?! James frantically asked.

"Trouble! We need to get as far from here as possible and get Brij to send some hunters down there before anybody gets killed," Rayna replied. "If we still have hunters in the country, that is."

"What do you mean by if it still has hunters?" James enquired.

"Trinidad is not the only place in the world with evil entities. Hunters does travel around the world to kill these things, but we are not a big operation. Six hunters make up the remainder of our family," Rayna responded.

"Then let me and Alister join in and help out," James pleaded.

"James! Enough!" Rayna shouted.

"But we just—" James was interrupted.

"You know how lucky Alister is to walk away tonight? How lucky we get that it was by him and not us? How lucky we get that Brij installed a pure iron crash bar in this truck?" Rayna stated. "Alister lucky he didn't get killed on the spot; most people freeze up and end up dying because they couldn't escape. We had nothing to repel that thing back there when we were on the beach. And if the crash bar wasn't pure iron, we would ah hit something solid instead of it turning to smoke and run off the road or flip the truck. And if we was lucky, me and you might have survived, but Alister was gonna go flying out the tray.

"I get yuh want to help. Trust meh, I know yuh think you doing the right thing, but facts are facts. If ulyuh wasn't here with me tonight and I wasn't driving Brij's truck, we would ah be dead. Just like the vagrant we see on the beach, and the people he say went missing in the bush. A willing attitude is not all it takes to be a hunter, else I would ah be one too," Rayna explained. Her rage calmed for her following words. "Make this the last time yuh even think about becoming a hunter. This is not ulyuh burden. This was Raphael's one. Please ah begging yuh," Rayna said as she turned to James. "Please stop!"

James looked at her for a moment. He heard her words and saw the pain in her eyes; he nodded at her and turned to face the front, not speaking a word for the rest of the drive.

Alister took out his phone and turned on his mobile data, doing some research for the rest of the ride home.

CHAPTER
11

Less than an hour later, Rayna drove up the driveway to her house. Brij, who was sitting outside on the porch, stood up when Rayna drove in faster than usual. Alister hopped out of the tray, and Rayna and James exited the vehicle soon after. "Widdi ass you doing in the tray?" Brij asked.

"Brij, we have a problem; I hada talk to yuh inside," said Rayna.

"Wait, you serious, Rayna? I was almost ghost chow; you really just gonna cut us out," Alister stated in disbelief.

"We don't have time to talk about this," Rayna informed Alister. Turning to Brij, she continued, "Any hunters on the island?"

"No, everybody occupied; why?" Brij questioned.

"There was a Churile…," Alister began.

"What?!" Rayna quickly turned around in shock.

Brij looked at Alister before grabbing Rayna by the shoulders. "Child, what the ass he talking about? Ent we say they not going to be hunters?" asked Brij furiously.

"I didn't say anything to them; how yuh know that?" Rayna asked Alister.

"I not as useless as you keep making me out to be," Alister responded.

Brij let go of Rayna and marched swiftly to Alister, grabbing him by the collar and pushing him against the truck. "Yuh feel is some kinda game?! Eh?! Yuh think we warning yuh cause we trying to hide something?!" Brij shouted.

Alister pushed Brij away forcefully by thrusting his palms into his chest. Rayna quickly got in Alister's way, ready to fight. "I go tell yuh what yuh not gonna fucking do is put yuh damn hands on me again, 'cause next time I'll—" James pulled Alister away mid-sentence.

"Rayna... Three ah ulyuh go inside," Brij sighed.

"Yes, sir," Rayna complied. Alister and James looked at them for a bit before agreeing to go inside.

The four assembled in the living room; Rayna, Alister, and James sat together on the sofa while Brij paced the space around them.

"Alright, explain what happened. Rayna, you say first," Brij instructed.

"Well, after we get food, we end up in Maracas 'cause I had carry the boys for a lil drive on the beach. Since Alister had some family friends in the village, he leave us and went to check them. Me and James went for food, but nowhere was open. The bar was closed, too, so we walked back by the village where the fishing boats come in and heard a woman's scream.

"We didn't really find anything, but I found it weird that it had nobody on the beach or the road. Nothing, except the vagrant who does be outside the bar," Rayna explained.

Brij stood with his arms folded and listened to Rayna recall the night's events.

Rayna continued, "The vagrant tell we how people started going missing and how he saw people go in the bush behind the food court and the bar. Some even get dragged into the bush. The man was shaking, afraid to go back to the other side of the beach. Unfortunately, we didn't realize he had a big hole in he chest, so he had bleed out and dead right dey."

Alister looked to James while Rayna spoke; James nodded 'yes' to confirm that her words were truthful.

"We didn't really wait around after that. We jumped in the truck and drove off. But we heard the scream again when we reached the lil hill at the beach entrance. Suddenly, Alister jumped in the tray out of nowhere. Then we saw it on the road, and I rammed it with the truck. The iron repel it, so we was good," Rayna finished.

"I am more concerned about why you say it was a Churile? Yuh wasn't with them according to Rayna; what yuh see?" Brij asked Alister.

"I hear about people seeing and hearing things from a family friend in the village, but nobody could say exactly what they see. When I was walking back, I heard a child crying, like a baby. And then I saw something move near the river that does run through that village. The hand was blueish-black and stained with something; I couldn't tell from where I was. I looked around for someone to help, but she was gone in the blink of an eye, moving like twenty feet in no time. Next thing I know, a woman in white was next to me; her hands and dress were bloody, and she grabbed my wrist and screamed," Alister answered.

"And what yuh do?" asked Brij.

"I run! What the fuck? If some demon-looking thing grabbed you and screamed, you going to stand up one place?" Alister remarked.

"Normally, yuh does be paralyzed by the fear. Yuh head saying move, but yuh body refuses to do it. So then wah happen after? Yuh just break free?" Brij questioned.

"No, I started praying," Alister replied.

"Praying doh work here. Evil wouldn't let yuh go free if you have faith in God," Brij explained.

"Exorcizamus te, omnis immundus spiritus—" Alister chanted.

Rayna flew off the chair, and Brij unfolded his arms. "What—" Brij exclaimed, shocked.

"Raphael wouldn't teach yuh that—" Rayna declared.

"He didn't," Alister stated, looking up at her with piercing eyes. "I keep trying to tell ulyuh I not as useless as yuh think."

"The Trini does peek out when yuh vex," Brij chuckled.

Alister looked at Brij, and he smiled. "What make yuh say Churile? From what yuh describe, it could be a few things: a woman in white, a Banshee, a flat-out ghost...," Brij exclaimed.

Alister raised his arm and showed Brij the red mark left on his forearm. Brij and Rayna walked over to Alister and held his hand, examining the reddish-black mark. "A ghost can't leave physical marks like this. Plus, the child crying is part of the lore for a Churile that the others don't have attached to them," Alister explained.

"And where yuh learn this?" Brij asked. "Not like yuh know yuh was gonna find one here and all the books with this kinda thing in Raphael library. So how yuh know this?"

"I didn't know at the time, but I figured it out on the way back," Alister replied.

"While yuh was in the tray?" Rayna enquired curiously.

"Yup," Alister responded.

"Damn," Rayna mumbled. "Brij yuh know this mean he go start to decay right," she stated as she pointed at the mark on Alister's arm.

"Wait, wait… Decay? Like his hand will rot off?" asked James frantically.

"I get touched by some heavy evil, James. It'll turn out the same way that Churile's body was: blue and black and rotten with dead flesh. If we doh kill it, it would take a few days to rot my entire body before I die," Alister informed him.

"Wow, wow, die?!" James exclaimed in disbelief.

Brij looked at Alister in the midst of the commotion; James was being overrun by emotion, while Alister had already made peace with the fact that he could die.

"Relax, nobody going to die, right Brij?" said Alister.

"Wah yuh mean? Why yuh watching me?" asked Brij.

"'Cause you know this would disappear if we kill the Churile," Alister replied.

"Or we could cut off the piece of flesh that rotted," Rayna suggested.

"No, sweetheart, you will cut nothing. I quite like my hands," Alister remarked.

"We have no hunters here right now. The time it would take for them to come back, it might be too late. Yuh need to do something now while is just a lil spot. Wait too long, and yuh could be looking at taking off the entire arm altogether," Rayna declared.

"It must have something else we could do!" James remarked.

"Nope. You boys not going to hunt, sorry," Brij stated. He turned and walked into the next room.

"Wait, that's it? He says no, and we're just supposed to live with it?" asked James.

"James, you promised—" said Rayna.

"This is my family you're talking about. I not gonna let him rot to death and be quiet about it," James gushed.

"That's enough... Let's just go upstairs. I think we've had enough for one day, bro," Alister said softly.

Alister and James turned, walked into the next room, and headed upstairs to the bedroom. Alister sat on the bed and stayed quiet for a bit; James paced the room holding his head frantically.

EXORCIZAMUS TE

***

Rayna walked into the room with Brij; he was holding the phone they had used earlier when they were spying on the boys through the hidden camera on the wall outlet.

***

Alister closed his eyes and placed his palm hovering over the bruise on his arm left by the Churile's touch. He whispered, "Exorcizamus te, omnis immundus spiritus. Omnis Satanica potestas, omnis incursio infernalis adversii. Omnis congregatio et secta diabolica, ergo, draco maledicte ecclesiam tuam. Secura tibi facias libertate servire, te rogamus, audi nos." Alister touched his palm to the bruise, and a black smoke appeared from beneath his skin. He bent over in pain; James stood frozen in shock and watched Alister as the smoke faded away. Alister removed his palm and found the mark had disappeared from his hand.

***

Rayna and Brij looked at each other in shock. "Did he just—" Rayna began.

"I have never seen anyone use the chant to cleanse themselves like that... Only ever on weapons," Brij gulped. *Who the fuck is this boy? I think I starting to get why Raphael picked him.*

Brij and Rayna were still watching the video feed when Alister looked straight at the hidden camera and raised his hand to show them that it was good as new. "Nice try with the camera, Rayna. Next time, be more discreet," Alister spoke toward the camera.

"The bitch knew... He show we he had the key on purpose," Brij said.

CHAPTER 12

James followed Alister's eye-line; he looked at the hidden camera Brij had plugged into the wall earlier that day when they had arrived. "What? What camera?" James exclaimed.

Alister pointed to the wall outlet. "The nightlight she plugged in is actually a hidden camera. I found it strange that she would just come and plug in a random light. Most people would just give it to us in the event we wanted to use it. Plus, it had outlets all over the room; one was closer to her, and the other outlets were more convenient. But to plug it directly in view of us… I just found it suspicious. Think about it, why would people who hunt ghosts and shit have a nightlight? I figured maybe it was something to protect us, like what Uncle Raph would give us. I did some research on it, only to find out it was just used to spy, so I gave them something to see," Alister explained.

Brij and Rayna entered the room, and Alister and James turned to them upon entering. "So, you does spy on everybody who visits, or we just special?" Alister smirked.

"How long yuh know?" asked Brij.

"Within a few minutes. You're not the only person with trust issues," Alister remarked.

"I not gonna apologize, just so yuh know. Yuh in my house, and what I do in my house is my business," Brij stated.

"Fair enough," Alister replied.

"Now, hand over Raphael's key. Keep the charm; it go protect yuh. I just want the pentagram on the keychain," Brij demanded.

"No," Alister immediately responded.

The tension in the room grew thick as Brij approached him. "Say that again?" Brij said.

"Listen, Raphael leave this for me; you don't get to demand anything," Alister declared.

Brij slapped Alister with all the force he could muster; Alister's ear rang, and his vision blurred for a moment. "Leme tell yuh sumn boy. I is not one ah yuh lil friend, yuh hear what I tell yuh." Brij grabbed Alister by his collar and threw a right hook busting open the side of his cheek.

James attacked Brij but was quickly taken down by Rayna, who threw him onto the floor and stomped on his neck, squeezing tight with her foot.

Brij pulled Alister off the bed, "Doh bleed on my fucking sheets. Yuh doh wash nothing here!" Headbutting Alister, Brij threw him out the room door, where he bashed into the adjacent wall in the hallway, blood lightly splatting on the walls. Alister was knocked out cold on the floor. James gasped for air, and his eyes began to roll back in his head. Rayna took her foot off of him; he coughed and struggled to breathe for a while.

Brij riffled through Alister's bag and found the charm that belonged to Raphael. Brij walked over to James and kicked him in his face, knocking him out too.

***

Hours later, Alister and James woke up in bed. Alister's head was bandaged, and James wore a nose splint. Brij's kick had broken it when he had knocked James out earlier.

Rayna entered the room with a phone in hand, looking at the video feed to their room.

"Good, y'all awake; how yuh feeling?" Rayna asked.

Alister sat upright on the bed and looked at Rayna before turning to James and shaking him lightly. "You ok, bro?" Alister questioned.

James slowly opened his eyes and groaned. "What the fuck happened?" asked James.

"Sorry Brij do that to ulyuh," Rayna exclaimed.

"Sorry? You for real, Rayna! You didn't do anything. If anything, you help Brij assault us," Alister retorted.

"You chose to answer the man back in he own house and talk about he grandson's son. I couldn't help that," Rayna responded.

"That's some bullshit; we leaving," Alister declared.

"Look, don't be hasty, aite. Just recover good first, then if you want, you could leave," Rayna told him.

"The moment we stepped foot in this house, we got beaten, shot at, insulted, and assaulted again. No thanks, I don't want to see this family again," Alister replied.

"Just so yuh know, Brij took back Raphael's charm," Rayna told the boys.

"He had no right! One ah these days, Brij go get what coming to him for what he do we. Keep the charm for all I care. I taking my cousin and staying as far away from this fucking place as possible," stated Alister.

"Suit yuhself," Rayna grumbled before leaving the room.

Alister turned to James. "You feeling ok?" Alister repeated.

"My head is killing me, but I go live," James replied.

"I'll call a taxi; let's just get out of this place," Alister announced. Alister got off the bed, walked over to the window, unlocked the safety, slid it open slightly, and looked outside.

EXORCIZAMUS TE

***

Rayna came down the stairs and found Brij sitting in the next room with a duffle bag on his lap. "Brij, they gonna leave," Rayna notified him.

Brij turned his attention to her. "Why? Because I buss he ass for talking back to meh?" asked Brij.

"Might have sumn to do with it," Rayna responded, stepping into the room and sitting on the sofa's armrest.

"They playing with things they have no business being around. I like the boys, inno, but this had nothing to do with them. This is a family matter, end of the story," Brij declared.

"You needed to knock them out, though?" Rayna questioned.

"Them young people these days doh know they damn place. Yuh in my house, interfering with my family issues and want to be getting on so?" Brij retorted.

"Yuh know they only want to help, right? Yuh didn't have to buss up he head so. Look yuh even break James' nose, and he didn't do anything," Rayna remarked.

"Enough! Listen to meh, young lady. Yuh letting yuh emotions chain up yuh head. I like them boys, and I loved Raphael. Yuh think it easy for me to treat the people he cared about like this? I hada do what I hada do and forget how I feel about it! Daz the job; yuh damn well know is a death sentence to involve these boys in this shit. Six hunters we have remaining after the thirteen others got killed doing this. Yuh know I refuse to send you in the field for this same reason, at least not without me out there with yuh.

"Yuh is a child, and I will not send yuh to dead, not you or them boys. I hard on yuh because it's my duty, the same way Raphael should ah be hard on them, but he wasn't and look where it bring them. Yuh know damn well them boys could ah dead last night in Maracas.

Raphael shouldn't have sent them here. Then they would ah never be there with you, and they would ah continue to live a good life away from this—" Brij was interrupted.

"Yuh wrong. Krampus found them; they didn't go to it. They were not with Uncle Raphael when it happened. If he wasn't hunting it, they wouldn't be here today. This wasn't out of some revenge thing. Raphael saw something we clearly don't; he chose Alister over he own son, Ravi, to carry out his legacy. That must mean something to yuh; I sure it digging at yuh," Rayna stated.

Brij looked at Rayna with a blank expression. "I know, child... But the work is almost done. After generations of this family fighting and losing so much of us, we are this close to the end. Once we banish Quattuor Equites off the face of the earth, then we could seal away the evil that roams this planet for good this time," Brij declared.

At that moment, Alister and James made their way down the stairs and entered the room with Rayna and Brij. Brij and Rayna stood up and turned to the boys. "We about to head out; we not going to be a problem for you anymore, Brij," Alister told him.

"Ulyuh doh need to leave yuh know," said Brij calmly.

"I think we've had enough. I doh want any more trouble, aite? Thanks for letting us stay here for a day, but we go be on we way now. I honestly just need to get as far from this family as I can, no offense," Alister responded. Alister and James turned and walked out the door, waving goodbye as they walked past them. Rayna and Brij looked on as they left, not saying a word.

Alister and James made their way down the track, and the iron gates unlocked once they reached the end. They looked back at the gate; Alister gazed up at the camera and shook his head in disappointment. The taxi pulled up a moment later. After tossing their bags in the trunk, Alister and James got in the back and told the driver to take them to the airport. Driving off soon after, Alister took one last look at the cameras by the gate and glared into them with piercing eyes as the car drove off.

CHAPTER 13

Brij and Rayna packed bags in the house while Rayna simultaneously looked at the footage from the camera at the gate. "They seem pissed," Rayna muttered.

"Worry about that later; right now, we have no hunters and a Churile on the loose in Maracas. Yuh know what that means, right!?" asked Brij.

"Yeah, if we kill it, we will draw out the harbinger and be one step close to Eques Famis, but we can't take on that. The Churile is the last of its line before the harbinger shows. We can barely do something about this—" Rayna responded.

"No, not we. I can do something about this. I might have retired to research, but I was still the best hunter of my time. But you, young lady, need to stay close; no trying to be a hero when we go," said Brij sternly. "I already call the hunters to come back; by the time the harbinger shows up, they will take care of that."

"Yes, sir," Rayna answered as she grabbed a shotgun and packed it into the duffle bag.

***

Alister and James were sitting in the car on the way to the airport when James turned to Alister and remarked, "Well, that was a horrible experience!"

Alister chuckled, "Really? 'Cause I was having a blast!"

"I am so sorry they took Raphael's charm from you," James sadly exclaimed.

Alister looked at James and smirked. Reaching into his t-shirt, he pulled out a charm from around his neck that was attached by a black cord. "You mean this?" he asked.

James' eyes widened. "You stole it back?" James enquired.

"Nope, it never left my person," Alister replied.

"How? Bro, Brij knocked you the fuck out. You were bleeding on the ground, and he went through your bag and took it. I saw him do it," James declared.

"You saw him take the copy I made. At the time, I had no idea it would come in handy like this. When I snagged it off Raphael's body, I expected Ravi to ask for it, so I made a new version for myself based on what Ravi told us in Switzerland. The mini mason jars were easy to find. I bought some holy water, and salt is easily accessible. I didn't have time to find a wooden carved sword or an iron crowbar to put on, so I improvised. A wooden ring and an iron one," Alister explained as he wiggled his fingers in front of his face. "They said you just need these things on you; didn't say it needed to be on the key chain. I found a cool silver sword pendant, but Raphael's charm had something Ravi's and Adelheid's didn't. This star-looking thing is called a pentagram. The version on Uncle Raphy's charm was different. I looked it up; it is a symbol of protection. Since this was unique to Raphael's, I didn't want to leave it to chance. I was sure Ravi might have asked for it if he ever saw it, so I made a copy. I found a good jeweler who cast a mold and made one for me. This happened while the family was mourning back home, and we knew we would come here. I didn't have time to make you one, but I will have one ready when we get back home. We just have one more thing to do before we leave," Alister smiled mysteriously.

"What's that?" asked James curiously.

"We are going to hit Raphael's library," Alister announced.

"Are you insane?" James remarked.

"They have no hunters here. So, I am willing to bet that means they will have to go to Maracas themselves to deal with the Churile," Alister whispered. "We will sneak into the house and enter the library once they leave. Nobody will even know. It's not like we need to take anything out of there. We just have to take pictures of the pages. It's an hour's drive to and from the beach; assuming they finish the job in seconds, we have two hours to get what we need and bail," Alister stated.

"Are you forgetting the cameras at the gate? How are we supposed to sneak inside?" James voiced.

"We don't; those cameras are our alibi. We wait till they leave, approach the gate, talk to the cameras, pretend like we think they are home, and say we left a phone or something in the house. When he doesn't answer, we'll jump the gate and break in," Alister replied.

"You really think we could break into a house? You know we have no idea how to pick a lock, right?" James kept his voice down so the taxi driver would not overhear their conversation while he listened to the radio.

"We don't need to pick a lock; I unlocked the window to the room we were in before we left," Alister smirked.

James remembered when Alister did that. "So, that's why you looked outside? A reason to unlock the window?"

"One, Brij was still spying, so yes, I did it to make sure it didn't seem suspicious rather than just unlocking it. And two, I needed to know where the window was, so when we came back, we knew which one to try, saving us the time needed to figure it out then," Alister remarked.

"You knew you were going to do this back then?" asked James in awe.

"Our old plan was useless 'cause we needed to wait for them to be asleep. But as long as we were there, Brij would be on our asses. So, that whole 'I never want to see this family again' was just a show to sell him on us really leaving, a fun little distraction to hide what I was really doing. The reason I didn't let you in on this plan is that he caught you lying from a mile away before, but he couldn't read me the same way. The last thing to cross his mind is that we have a copy of the key and a way into his house without causing suspicion," Alister explained.

"True, but how are you going to account for the time we spent there?" James enquired.

"Damn, you're right. It would still be odd that we spent two hours there and then left," said Alister.

"I think I have it. We can say we tried waiting for them to come back. Leave a note on the door and say we wanted to apologize while we were there and we waited for them, but it got late, and we bolted to catch our flight," James exclaimed.

"That's brilliant! Damn, what would I do without you, bro?" asked Alister.

"Let's not find out," James replied as he and Alister bumped fists.

"Hey, drive, they would have airport rental vehicles, right?" Alister asked.

"I not too sure about the airport, inno. But I could tell yuh where to go," the driver replied.

"Perfect, but food first; I could do with some doubles this early in the morning, yes," Alister stated. He turned to James and said, "We have a day to kill; Rayna and them wouldn't leave till the night."

"How do you know?" questioned James.

"I read up on it. The Churile appears after the sun sets; most likely, they would leave closer to the night. We could grab some food, get a car, camp outside the gate and watch for when they leave," said Alister.

"Sounds like a plan," James agreed.

CHAPTER
14

Alister and James stopped off at a doubles stand, excited to taste the Trinidadian delicacy again after so many years. Alister walked to the stand and ordered, "Three with slight."

The doubles vendor quickly put together two bara: a fried dough dressed with chickpeas and topped with condiments - cucumber chutney, chadon-beni chutney, roasted pepper, tamarind chutney, and pepper sauce. Alister and James were handed all three. Alister went to the taxi and handed one to the driver to eat with them. With their mouths watering, Alister and James used the bara to scoop up the chickpeas and condiments and took their first bite. James uttered a sound of pure joy at the taste of one of the best doubles he had ever had. Even though they made this at home, there was no other experience like standing at a food stall and eating freshly made doubles.

Alister slowly chewed and looked confused; he swallowed and turned to James. "Bro, how's yours tasting?" he mumbled quietly.

"This so good!" James responded.

"Bro, mine taste like cardboard, like no flavor at all," Alister remarked.

"Try mine," James said, switching his with Alister's, and they finished each other's doubles. James looked at Alister and saw him struggling not to spit the food out. He noticed that Alister had almost thrown up in his mouth twice, trying to swallow the food. "Yours taste really good, a lil better than mine, actually; it had more roasted pepper than I got," James commented.

"Bro, I don't know. I feeling sick; that didn't really taste good. It had no taste like I was chewing a wet cloth," Alister stated.

"The pepper a little hot too, my lips tingling," James retorted.

"I not feeling anything," said Alister.

"Try one with heavy pepper, 'cause that roasted pepper tasted so good," James suggested.

Alister turned to the doubles vendor and ordered another with more pepper this time. In a few seconds, he was handed another; Alister took a bite but still tasted nothing. "This much pepper should be burning my mouth. I can smell how hot it is," Alister exclaimed.

James looked at the bruise left on Alister's hand after he had cleansed the black mark of the Churile's touch. "You think that some have something to do with it?" he asked.

Alister also looked at the faded mark on his hand and replied, "Could be? I think I should test it." Alister turned to the vendor again and asked, "I could get some more roast pepper? Like two big spoonfuls?"

"Huh, so much pepper? You does shit fire, bhai?" the vendor chuckled, scooping two full spoons and adding them to the last remaining bara.

Alister made a little pouch with the bara and popped it into his mouth. He could smell the pungent aroma of the hot peppers while chewing, but he couldn't taste anything, swallowing it like it was nothing. The taxi driver got out, came to the stall, washed his hands, and took a drink from the cooler. "That doubles hot boy, wayyyy sah!" the driver remarked as he popped the cap off a cold bottled water and guzzled it down. Alister and James looked at each other with worried expressions.

James and the driver had one more doubles each before they left, while Alister returned to the taxi and examined his forearm. The blackened mark where the Churile touched him seemed to have faded since he used the chant to purify the spot back at Brij's. After finishing their food, James and the taxi driver returned to the car and drove to a car rental place twenty minutes away. Alister paid the driver, retrieved their bags from the trunk, and he and James entered the car rental establishment.

After waiting around and filling out the paperwork, Alister was able to rent a car for the day. They loaded the car with their bags, drove back to Endeavour, and pulled up a couple of houses down from Brij's gate as they scoped out the scene. Eventually, they drove by the entrance, and Alister caught a glimpse of Brij's truck still parked in the yard. So, they made a block, parked where they had a clear view of Brij's gate, and waited.

James turned to Alister half an hour into their wait and asked, "What if they don't go?"

"I think they have to; no other hunters are around, according to them. Remember, Rayna was in a hurry to come back and tell Brij. I don't think they would just do nothing. Especially after I almost got killed, and you guys found someone just before they died. What kind of hunters would they be if they let the deaths pile up? They don't strike me as cowards; I am willing to bet that Brij wouldn't just sit by and let people die while they wait for hunters. You saw them when we were leaving; they were packing bags. So, all the more reason to believe they would go back to Maracas. Uncle Raph was also a researcher, but he went to Switzerland to hunt Krampus. You really think they would ignore something like this in their own country, just an hour's drive from where they live?" Alister speculated.

"Let's hope you're right," said James.

Hours went by, and the cousins grew restless until they heard the sound of the iron gate creaking open. Alister and James sank into their seats, peeking just above the dashboard. They saw Rayna and Brij in the front seat of his truck, driving off toward the highway. Alister started the car and followed Brij's truck. "Where are we going?" James questioned.

"To make sure they are headed to the beach. The highway isn't that far from here; we can follow them till we get to it, and once we know for sure that they leave, then we can go back. Don't want to risk Brij and Rayna coming back early and finding us breaking into their house," Alister replied.

"Good idea; I rather not get beaten again like that. My head is still killing me," stated James.

Alister followed Brij at a safe distance behind him; Brij turned onto the highway and drove off in the direction of the beach. "Alright, it's go-time!" Alister declared.

Making a U-Turn, Alister drove back to Brij's house and parked in the same spot. They waited for a little over twenty minutes to avoid raising any suspicion when Brij eventually saw the video footage from the cameras.

Putting their plan into action, Alister and James took their bags out of the car and walked to the gate. Stepping into view of the camera, Alister waved and called out to Brij. He waited a bit and looked around; he turned to the camera again and claimed, "Our flight leaves soon. I really need my phone; I must have left it in the room. I'm coming in to get it."

The boys climbed over the gate, dropped their bags on the side of the walkway in the tall grass, and sprinted to the house.

"We don't have much time. In and out as quickly as we can; this is a long walk, but they have no cameras on this walkway. This could buy us a lot of time, plus the time it would take to 'look for the phone' and then walk back," Alister said while they ran.

"What happened to saying we waited for them as a way to buy more time?" James enquired.

"I'm making this up as I go, bro; it's about adapting to the situation. It seemed like a good plan then, but now that we are here, it feels real, and I'd rather not take the chance. The faster we get in and out, the better. Let's hurry," Alister motioned for James to follow him as he ran down the trail.

Alister saw the marker for the room they stayed in. James gave him a boost to the lower roof outside their room, and Alister pulled James up once he got onto it. The window he left open was still unlocked, so they climbed in quickly. Alister hurriedly looked for the hidden camera, but it wasn't plugged into the wall anymore. "Oh, thank God. Brij took out the camera. That's one less thing to worry about," Alister mumbled. They swiftly ran into the hall and down to the locked room. Alister reached into his shirt and pulled out Raphael's original key, placing it in the lock and turning. The lock clicked open and fell to the floor; James and Alister swiftly entered the room and closed the door behind them.

The room was huge and filled with books, top to bottom; Alister and James felt uneasy. Their plans didn't account for this many books to choose from.

"Bro, I don't think we have enough time for all of this," James exclaimed.

"Nope, definitely not; any ideas?" asked Alister.

"I see a desk over at the other end of the room; let's see what's on there?" James suggested.

Alister and James ran over quickly to a messy pile of books and pages scattered on the desk.

"Ok, not good; none of this is even in English," stated James.

"Wait, that's it. Do you remember when we entered the room before we left? Brij was saying something about 'The End.' He said something Equites... Qatar Equites? You look here, and I'll check the shelves. Find out what that means," said Alister as he disappeared into the shelves.

Both scanned through books quickly, most of them without names on the spines. Alister was forced to randomly pull each book out of the row to peak at the cover. James rifled through the mess on the table, not a word of English among the pages. Their time was running out, and Alister began to panic; there must have been over three thousand books in that room.

"Alister!" James called out, "Quattuor Equites! Is that what they said?"

Alister came running to the desk. "I think so!" Alister said, panting.

"Quick, start recording; there are a lot of pages to flip through here," James declared.

Alister and James flipped through the entire book, stopping only when they saw a familiar picture, a sketch of Krampus. The cousins looked at each other. "This must be what Brij was talking about; no way that Krampus is in this by coincidence," said Alister, continuing to flip through as fast as they could. After recording the book, they hurriedly left the room, locked the library door, and climbed out the window.

Jumping off the lower roof and back to the ground, they sprinted to the gate, having achieved their goal. They grabbed their bags from the tall grass and hopped over the gate again. The evening sky began to dim as Alister looked up at the camera, shook his phone, and talked to the camera, saying that he had found it. Waving goodbye, they left and returned to the parked car.

CHAPTER
15

Alister tossed the keys to James and instructed, "You drive. I want to get started on this book. I'm dying to know what Brij meant by 'The End' and what the hell 'Quattuor Equites' is." Alister moved over to the passenger seat, took his phone out, and began trying to translate the text using his phone.

"Where to? The airport?" asked James.

"Yes, definitely the airport; we want to be in a nice public space in case Brij finds out we broke into the library. I'll check the flights. We can get the first one out of here," Alister responded.

"Got it," James replied while setting the GPS in the car to guide them to the Piarco International Airport.

***

Meanwhile, Brij and Rayna arrived in Maracas. Their first stop was at the bar and the food court, only to realize that both places were still closed.

"It's just like yesterday; nothing was open," Rayna commented.

"It still have people on the beach, but barely. Place done dark, we hada find this thing and move fast," Brij declared. He looked behind him to reverse the truck and turned to head back to the village. There, he noticed a man and his child drying off with a towel near their car in the parking lot behind the bar. The child was holding his father's pant leg while he dried off his head with a towel. Suddenly, a noise diverted his attention to the bushes behind them.

Realizing the truck had stopped moving, Rayna turned to Brij. Following his gaze, she turned to the child and the father in the parking lot. "Brij, that is where the vagrant say people were getting grabbed—" she whispered.

"Go, now!" Brij ordered.

Rayna reached into the duffle bag between them on the seat and pulled out a shotgun. She hopped out of the truck and ran to the man and his child. "Aye, boy! Ulyuh move from dey!" Rayna shouted while running toward them, concealing the shotgun behind her.

The man looked at his feet; the child wasn't holding onto his pant leg anymore. Frantically looking around and calling out to his son, the man heard a rustling in the bushes and took off in that direction.

"No! Doh go dey!!!" Rayna yelled. The man ran through the bushes and into a shallow river. There he found his son standing on the other side of the riverbank. Running across the water to his son, he grabbed his hand and picked him up quickly. A cold hand grabbed him by the wrist, and he screamed. The Churile, with its hair shrouding its face and its pale white eyes peeking through the strands of hair, released a demonic scream that paralyzed the man. A reddish black bruise grew from his wrist, where the Churile gripped tightly and trailed up his arm.

Rayna racked the shotgun, held it to the head of the Churile, and fired. With the weapon in one hand now, she grabbed the man and his child with the other as it disappeared into thin air. Seeing the man panicked and struggling to breathe, Rayna slapped him to draw his attention. She then told him to take his son, get in their car, and leave the area immediately. Rayna helped them across the shallow river and hurried them to their vehicle. The man had questions for Rayna, but she sternly warned him not to ask. She convinced him to leave without the answers he wanted but told him that he should stop by the truck parked just up ahead.

When Rayna returned to the truck, Brij got out and went to the man and his child. He took the man's hand, whispered the incantation used to cleanse objects, and placed his hand over the man's arm, causing it to heal instantly.

"Get in yuh car and go up the road; doh tell a soul what happen here, yuh hear meh!" Brij instructed.

The man nodded his head 'yes,' got in the car, and drove off immediately.

Brij turned to Rayna and asked, "Yuh ok? Yuh hurt?"

"I good," Rayna replied.

"Yuh sure?" Brij asked again.

"I good, I good," Rayna repeated.

"Aite, well tell meh, he was right?" Brij enquired.

"Yeah, Alister was right. It was ah Churile self," Rayna answered. Just then, a demonic scream came from the river; Brij and Rayna turned toward the eerie sound.

"How the iron dust rounds work?" asked Brij.

"Wonders," Rayna replied.

"Good, use the rounds instead of a piece of iron; they fast, but we guns faster," Brij stated.

"How we gonna kill this one?" questioned Rayna.

"It too late to find the body, not in this darkness; we hada find out if she kill sheself or if she died during the pregnancy to become a Churile. Yuh say it attack out on the road when you ram it with the truck, right? Means the body could be anywhere from the village to that point; too much ground to cover. We heading to the village and question everybody who go talk to we. We need to find out who she was before she died so we go know how to kill it. If she commit suicide, we in shit. We go have to find the body. But if she get killed, at least they go know where she buried or where she died. It go narrow down the search. Lewe go," Brij explained before he got back in the truck with Rayna, drove up the street, and headed to the village.

***

While Alister and James were still on their way to the airport, he deciphered some of the text and began explaining to James. "Quattuor Equites is Latin; it means the four Horsemen," Alister began.

"You mean like 'THE' four Horsemen? Of the apocalypse?" James asked in shock.

"Yes and no… The book is about the four Horsemen: Famine, War, Conquest, and Death. Except it's not the stories we know. They are not the manifestation of these things, but rather it's what brings forth the effects of the horsemen. Krampus, for example, the lore said they appeased Krampus for good weather and

147

crop yield. Also, we tangled with it, and it left Alyssa in a coma that we couldn't wake her from. The Horseman of Conquest achieves this by using pestilence as one of its weapons. Krampus didn't just make Alyssa sick; it made the land itself sick. No crops could grow, no good weather could come. It's beyond just sickness and a plague; it's not targeting humans; it's a plague on the earth itself," Alister explained.

"You know, I always wondered about the face of Krampus; it wore a skull mask like those plague doctors you see in movies," James commented.

"Exactly, this is where it originated," Alister told him.

"What else does it say?" asked James.

"Well, each Horseman has a Harbinger, a warning sign of the horsemen itself. Think of the horsemen as the captains and the Harbingers as the vice-captains. It says Krampus was a Harbinger, and the Horseman of Conquest is far more deadly than the Creature of the Yuletide," Alister continued.

"You mean that thing was the lesser of the two evils? Then I don't even want to know what the horsemen are like," James remarked.

"Thankfully, the Horsemen only show when the Harbingers are annihilated. This means if we had killed Krampus back in Switzerland, we would be ass deep in something much worse right now. There is a reason they are called the Horsemen of the Apocalypse. Krampus only affected a village, but it says the horsemen can disrupt entire hemispheres with their very presence on earth," Alister stated.

"You mean to tell me Brij and his family are hunting these things? What do they intend to do?" James wondered.

"I haven't gotten that far yet. This is just the intro page," Alister answered.

"Well, keep reading; we're almost at the airport," said James.

CHAPTER 16

Rayna and Brij entered the village. People were seen hurrying off the street and into their houses as the darkness of the night descended. "Keep the pistol on yuh. The shotgun go draw too much attention. Use the pistol with the suppressor and use the iron rounds. Until we find the Churile's location, we moving quietly. Doh draw no attention to yuhself, and take a walkie-talkie while yuh go question the residents. But stay close enough to me and doh engage without me, yuh hear meh?" Brij said sternly.

"Yes, sir, I understand," Rayna replied.

"Good. Start on the right side of the street; I will go on the left. We go work we way up, house by house," Brij instructed. Rayna and Brij attached suppressors at the barrel of their handguns, took a couple magazines of iron rounds, and concealed the guns inside their thick denim jackets. They got out of the truck and split up, going to opposite sides of the street to speak to the villagers.

***

Alister and James pulled up in the airport's parking lot; Alister was still busy translating the book line by line. "James, listen to this. Eques Famis means the Horseman of Famine. This isn't word for word; some of the translations are jumbled and not very precise. But this is essentially what it says: every evil being that ever existed on earth came from the horsemen. When the horsemen roam the Earth, the evil surrounding it creates harbingers of its will, monsters that wield the power of the horseman they descended from. Krampus was a harbinger of the Horseman of Conquest, Eques Victoriae. Its power was that of pestilence, not just of humans, but the earth itself. It says wherever they go, they bleed the planet, and those wounds create more evil, and the cycle continues.

"The further down the line it goes, the weaker the creatures are, but they all share the ability of the horsemen. Once the harbingers are killed, the horsemen will roam the earth again until another harbinger is born. Killing a horseman will not vanquish its lineage, but it will strip them of the abilities of the horseman, making them much easier to kill," Alister explained.

"I can see why Brij is set on going after the horsemen," James exclaimed.

"The first one I read was Eques Victoriae, the Horseman with Krampus as its Harbinger. The next one is Eques Famis, the Horseman of Famine. We know famine means a scarcity of food. But this one is much deeper than that. It says this horseman is the weakest of the four, but it racks up a death toll second only to the Horseman of Death, Eques Mortis. Famine's power strips you of your ability to consume certain foods, mainly salt. Once you are unable to eat salt, it has a ripple effect causing malnutrition, and eventually, you lack the ability to stomach anything altogether. First, you won't be able to eat salt, then it strips you of your tastebuds, slowly taking away your ability to stomach food on the whole. So, famine isn't the lack of food. It's the lack of the ability to eat—" Alister continued.

"Alister—" James interjected.

"I know, it's exactly what's happening to me," Alister agreed.

"No…," James sighed.

"That's not what I am worried about right now. Look at this," Alister said as he pointed to a sketch in the book. "This is what I saw back in the village. The death omen of the harbinger of Eques Famis is a Churile, much like the Yule Goat is to Krampus. It seems each of the harbingers has a death omen that shows up before it," Alister continued.

"Fuck!" James exclaimed.

"I am still waiting for this page to be translated. We have a few minutes till it's done processing," Alister told James.

"Are we just going to sit here and do nothing?" James enquired.

"I don't want to, but if we go there and get someone else killed, Brij will have our heads, especially if we let something happen to Rayna. As much as I want to go, a part of me thinks we just need to sit this one out," Alister responded.

"And what does the rest of you think?" asked James.

Alister turned to James. "The rest of me thinks Raphael wouldn't let them go alone if he was here," Alister answered.

James smirked and started the car.

MARACAS BAY DARK RIVER

***

Rayna and Brij had no luck; none of the residents would speak to them. Afraid to step outside their own homes, the residents warned Rayna and Brij to leave the village immediately.

As Rayna and Brij approached Asha's minimart, she exclaimed, "Brij, yuh remember when Alister said he was by a family friend who tell him about people seeing and hearing things? This is where he was talking about."

"Good, lewe hope they still in a talking mood," Brij remarked as he and Rayna walked off the street and onto a little dirt trail that led up to the minimart's window, which was still open. "Pleasant good night!" Brij called out.

Asha came to the window. "Hi?" she said as she peeked through the tiny window.

"Miss Asha, you mind if we come inside for a chat? I'm Rayna, and this is my great-grandfather, Brij. I am a friend of Alister's; he was here last night," Rayna stated.

"He ok?" asked Asha worriedly.

"Not really, we hoping yuh could help we out," Brij answered.

"Curtis, open the door!" Asha shouted. The door opened, and Curtis invited them inside.

"What happen to that child?" asked Asha frantically.

"He told us about how people were seeing and hearing things in the village," Brij explained.

Curtis and Asha exchanged worried looks. "Yes, oh gosh, doh tell me it get him," Asha's voice cracked as she said this.

"No, but he almost get killed, and from what we understand, people dying here and going missing a lot recently. We could help, but you need to give us as much information as you can. Anything at all, no matter how small," Rayna stated.

"That's all we know. We just hear villagers talk about hearing screams and seeing things in the village, but nobody really ever say what it was," Curtis answered.

"How long since this began happening?" asked Brij.

"About two months? Same time the bake and shark shed close down, and the bar closed right after," Asha informed them.

"Why did it close? Ulyuh know?" questioned Brij.

"Yeah, my mother has a stall in the food court. She say people were complaining about the food, saying it eh tasting good, like it doh have any taste. After a few days, people stop buying altogether 'cause they couldn't stomach it. Same thing with the bar; the food and drinks had plenty of complaints," Asha explained.

"Yeah, I used to work dey before it close down. People say the food and thing used to taste like wet napkin, and the rum was like drinking water, telling we how we putting too much ice in we drinks," Curtis added.

"Ulyuh ever taste the food?" asked Rayna.

"Yeah, we does make all the time. When we go by ma in the morning, she bake and shark used to taste good. I doh know what them people complaining about," Asha responded.

"Anybody in the village complain about the food or just outsiders?" asked Brij.

"Not that we know of," Asha answered.

"Oh wait, we child, Maleah. She having trouble eating for a while now; all she does eat is fruits and vegetables," said Curtis.

"She does sleep most of the day?" asked Brij.

"Y— Yeah, how yuh know that?" Curtis enquired.

"Where the child now?" Brij immediately asked.

Curtis and Asha showed Brij to the room where Maleah was sleeping. Brij sat on the edge of the bed and felt her skin; it was cold to the touch.

"How long this child like this?" questioned Brij.

"About a little over a month and a half? We didn't notice it until she started taking fruits from the minimart instead of snacks; she love ah sugar," Curtis exclaimed.

"What happen to she?" Asha asked in a panic.

"She slowly losing she ability to eat. By chance, the sales on your fruits gone up since the bar and food court closed? Specifically, the fruits," Brij enquired.

"She losing she ability to eat?! Oh God! Meh child go be ok?!" Asha panicked.

"Madam, I need you to focus. For the sake of that child, yes or no on the fruits?" Brij repeated.

"Yes," Curtis answered.

"One person or multiple?" asked Brij.

"A lot of people from the village, actually," Curtis replied.

"Fuck. It not haunting one person; it going after everybody, but it doh sound like it after people in the village. Yuh say people does see and hear things, right, but ulyuh had any deaths inside the village?" Brij probed.

"A few in the village, but people who visit sometimes die too. Police come a few times to investigate dead bodies and missing people," Curtis answered.

"So, is not vengeful spirit type shit; it's some other motive," Rayna said to Brij.

"Any ladies died here recently?" Brij asked.

"People pass away a lot; this year alone, we had four deaths in the village," Curtis responded.

"Any suicides or murders or any violent deaths or anything like that that stood out?" questioned Brij.

"No, not really. This place doh have that kinda thing; everybody here so peaceful," Curtis replied.

"No, wait, ent the lady further up the hill get hit by a car? That count?" Asha corrected Curtis.

"Who hit she?" Rayna enquired.

"Well, they never really see, but they find she husband on the road. They say she went flying off the road and end up somewhere in the river from on top the hill," Asha answered.

"Poor lady was pregnant, too. Them muddass drunk drivers, she was a nice woman too, inno. She rel wanted a child," said Curtis.

"I doh know if is true, but yuh know how people does talk. They say she had a lil outside man. But the man didn't know she was married, and he come and catch them together and run them over. But dais just old talk them does carry on in the village; the police say it was most likely a drunk driver," Asha announced.

Brij and Rayna looked at each other. "I think we have everything we need. The child gonna have trouble eating for a bit, but we gonna fix it. The less we tell ulyuh, the better.

Trust meh, yuh doh want to know. Just trust that we will ensure your child will be safe by the end of the night. And stay inside," Brij ordered as he took his walkie-talkie and gave it to Curtis. "If yuh see or hear anything, use this and tell me. We go be around the village; the range for this should reach we while we here. Doh worry about Alister either; he and the child in the same situation, so once she good, he go be good too," Brij comforted them.

Brij and Rayna got up and left; they swiftly looked around and got back into their truck.

CHAPTER

17

Alister and James listened to their gut instinct and drove down the highway on route to Maracas Bay. Alister finally got the translation of the page he and James were waiting on. He browsed through, whispering to himself while he read quickly. "No...," he mumbled.

"What?" James asked curiously.

"The Churile is a death omen of the harbinger; it's definitely from the line of Eques

Famis. Listen to this, a Churile is the spirit of a woman who died during pregnancy. Dressed in white and with hair covering her face, she roams after dark, wailing with the fetus of her unborn child in her arms while the child cries to be fed. Churiles attack men mainly, luring them and even sleeping with them, then killing them before the night ends. However, they feed off of the life of children. They slowly drain their life force to give life to the child they never had but are unable to bring their child to life for eternity.

"Churiles, however, grow vengeful in the presence of pregnant women; they possess mothers to be and kill the child in their womb, leading to miscarriages. It says that the power of the death omen slowly strips away the taste of food, and foods with salt become like mush that taste of nothingness. With time, the lack of salt will cause nausea, vomiting, and dizziness. Soon after that, the final stages begin: the body goes into shock, eventually leading to a coma followed by death," said Alister.

"You've only been exposed to it for one day, yet you still managed to eat. So, as long as you keep eating, you will be fine, even if it tastes like nothing," James commented.

"It's not me I'm worried about," Alister stated. James looked over at him for a moment. "Aunty Asha has a kid who spends most of her days sleeping and can't eat home-cooked meals," Alister told him.

"Oh my God—" James exclaimed.

"And she's expecting another; she's pregnant," Alister shakily said.

James faced the road and floored the acceleration. "Does it say how to kill it?" James asked.

"Not yet, but there is something on how to stay alive if you encounter one. It says a Churile can't cross water. The other way to avoid it is a bit weird, but this is what it says: leave a pair of shoes behind, and the Churile will spend the night trying to put on the shoes," Alister continued.

"Really? Are you sure that's what it says?" James questioned, baffled by that statement.

"It may not be word for word, but that's definitely what is written in the book. It says these things don't know they are spirits; to them, this is just the natural cycle of life. They relive the agony of their death on a loop, not knowing they are dead until it rips away their humanity. All that remains is the will of the horsemen," Alister explained.

"We are just a few minutes out, according to the GPS. Can you find out how to kill it?" James suggested.

"It takes some time for the page to translate. I won't know for a little while," Alister informed James.

"Then what are we going to do!?" James grunted.

"We get to the village and keep Asha, Curtis, and that kid safe until Brij and Rayna deal with this thing. Hopefully, they can do that before we get there," Alister replied.

"Then we are going to need something to protect them. We don't exactly have an arsenal like Brij, and you only have one charm," said James.

"I'm aware, but we can't just do nothing, James!" Alister stated.

"Wait, Rayna said the crash bar was pure iron. She said if it wasn't, we would have crashed into the Churile, which means pure iron would repel it, right?" James wondered aloud.

"You're right! All we need to do is find something made from iron before we get there," Alister agreed.

"We don't have time to stop anywhere; look it up on the internet. Find out what household items are made of iron," James advised.

"On it," Alister replied.

***

Brij and Rayna sat in his truck; they were safe inside it because of the iron reinforcement Brij had custom-built into the vehicle. "No sign of it again; yuh think the iron rounds is what repelling it this long?" asked Rayna.

"For sure, but it shouldn't be gone for too long; it should have been back by now. Iron wouldn't repel it forever," Brij answered.

"You thinking what I thinking?" said Rayna.

"Yuh mean the old talk they tell we about? For sure, that could be it. It go explain why it not going after people in the village, and only outsiders like that man and he child," Brij responded.

"If it only killing outsiders, I wonder why the vagrant got attacked? I mean, I know he from this beach since I was small. He is not an outsider," Rayna stated.

"That digging at meh too; yuh have internet up here?" asked Brij.

"Yeah, my data always on," Rayna replied.

"Look up the lady who died. See if it make the news; maybe it have something we miss," Brij suggested.

Rayna filtered the search results, and sure enough, she found the article about the tragic death of a married couple. "Found it! She and she husband, a local fisherman, died in a car accident when a drunk driver lost control. The body of the woman was never found and was assumed to have washed away in the river that flows through the village and down the mountain. Huh, I guess dais how she follow we so far down the road. The bridge was right after where she appeared, and Churiles can't cross water," Rayna claimed.

"Yeah, but that river separates the village and the other side where the boats does come in. How she roaming across the water there, but she couldn't do it when you shot her earlier?" questioned Brij.

"We need to find the body," Rayna advised.

"Not until she shows up. Yuh have the shoes?" asked Brij.

"Right here in the bag," Rayna replied as she took out a pair of old sneakers.

The truck's windshield began to frost up. Suddenly, the temperature dropped, accompanied by the streetlamp's lights flickering. The Churile, holding a bloody fetus in her arms, appeared in front of the truck. She wailed demonically into the night. Brij took the shoes from Rayna and got out of the truck; Rayna also exited, drew her gun, and aimed at the Churile. Brij walked up with the pair of shoes in one hand and his gun in the other. Taking one step at a time, he inched forward, placed the shoes at the foot of the Churile, and backed away.

The Churile screamed, stooped to the floor, and attempted to slip her feet into the shoes, but it did not work. She attempted to do it over and over again. "Ok, child, it's trapped; we have till sunrise to find the body. Lewe move!" Brij exclaimed as he and Rayna turned, got back into the truck, and drove to the top of the river.

CHAPTER

18

James sped around the corner at the entrance of the beach, the car skating along the road. Its tires screeched and smoked as it turned into the road to the village. Alister and James pulled up by Asha's house. Ahead of them was a pair of torn-up shoes swinging on the powerline of the streetlamps. Alister looked at it for a moment and recalled that leaving a pair of shoes behind would save their lives in the event that the Churile attacked. Hearing James closing his door snapped Alister out of his thoughts, and they both hurried to the entrance of Asha's and Curtis's house.

Alister knocked at the door and called out to Asha, asking her to open up, but no one answered. Alister peeked through the window, trying to see passed the laced curtain. Seeing a bell near the window of the minimart, James decided to press it and give that a try. They both heard the bell from outside. A set of footsteps came hurrying to the door, and shortly after, Curtis quickly swung open the door.

"Alister? Yuh ok! Where the girl and the old man?" asked Curtis frantically.

"Yuh mean Rayna and Brij?" Alister enquired.

"Yeah, Brij, that was he name," Curtis responded. "Come inside quick; Asha now faint away. I was trying to carry she to the bed."

Alister hurried inside and rushed passed Curtis. "Where Aunty Asha? In the room?" Alister questioned.

"Yeah, she ly-down, she lil dizzy," Curtis told him.

"Yuh have a hammer?" Alister asked.

"Ah hammer? What yuh need a hammer for?" Curtis asked in a panic.

"For the iron; the head of the hammer make from pure iron," Alister explained.

"Ok, yeah, yeah, I have one. If is iron yuh need, I have an old pipe in the back of the house that is iron too, but it a lil rusty," Curtis informed him.

"All dah go work," said Alister.

Curtis ran to the bedroom and pulled a tool chest from under his bed, searched through, and found the hammer for Alister. Alister, James, and Curtis headed to the back of the house to locate the iron pipe. James used his phone's flashlight to brighten the way. Curtis leaned over the pile of garbage and broken appliances to search for the pipe.

Curtis braced himself on an old stove and called out, "Flash the light closer here; I feel like I not seeing." He spoke while he threw aside pieces of broken toys and scrap appliances in his search. The glass window of the stove's oven suddenly began to crackle; Curtis stopped and listened to the sound near his ear. James and Alister started to hear it, too. James turned the flashlight toward the stove, revealing the window being frosted in ice.

Alister and James exchanged looks quickly. "Everybody inside!" Alister screamed.

***

Brij and Rayna, walking along the riverbank, heard a voice in the distance. Rayna turned to Brij. "Yuh hear that?" she whispered.

***

Curtis saw the piece of iron while running back to the house, so he quickly paused to grab it. "I get it!" he yelled. He pulled it up from beneath some scraps of garbage and turned to continue running but came face to face with the Churile. Alister and James turned just before they got to the door and caught a glimpse of Curtis standing there, inches from the creature. The Churile grabbed Curtis' arm and wailed.

***

Brij and Rayna heard the demonic scream in the distance. No words were spoken; the two drew their guns and ran toward the sound. "What the hell? The Churile should have been trapped trying to put on the shoes!" Rayna grunted.

"Some asshole must be move it!" Brij retorted.

Curtis tried to lift the arm the Churile grabbed to swing the iron rod in self-defense, but he was much weaker than the creature. James and Alister rushed over to him; Alister threw the hammer at the Churile to repel it, hitting Curtis instead.

"Not me! Hit the jumbie!!" Curtis shouted, holding his leg where he was struck by the hammer's handle.

James grabbed the iron pipe from Curtis' hand and yanked it out, leaving shards of rusty iron in Curtis's palm. James quickly swung at the Churile but it vanished into smoke with a demonic cackle.

At the same time, Curtis yelled out in pain, holding out his bloody hand, riddled with shards of rusty iron piercing his palm.

"Oh shit!" James remarked while helping Curtis to his feet and running back to the house.

Alister ran to the other side of Curtis and picked up the hammer before helping James carry Curtis back inside.

"What the ass was that!?" Curtis shakily asked.

Alister and James helped him to the couch. "We need something to stop the bleeding; I need a cloth and some alcohol, Uncle Curtis," said Alister.

"Oh, God! I hada go get tetanus injection again? I doh like needle," Curtis cried out.

"Check the cabinets in the kitchen for rum, and look for a clean kitchen towel," James instructed Alister. He whispered, "Alright, time to put four years of Med school to the test."

Alister found a bottle of rum and several kitchen towels and brought them over. "Mr. Curtis, this going to hurt, but I need to wash out the wounds and pull these pieces of rust out of your hand, ok?" said James.

"Oh God oi, my hand done turning blue-black. The tetanus spreading, and that needle so big… Last time they wanted to chook me in meh ass. Who does get tetanus injection in dey ass?" Curtis panicked.

"Hold still; this is going to hurt. Ready?" asked James calmly.

"Noooo, time out, time out," Curtis shouted.

"The longer we take to do this, the higher the chances of infection will get," James informed him.

"It done infected! Watch this big blue-black mark on my hand. And oh God, Alister pelt meh with the hammer. My leg must be blue-black too! What the hell was that out dey?" Curtis wailed.

Alister sat beside him. "For Maleah and Aunty Asha's sake and your unborn child, we need you to calm down and let James fix your wounds. I will explain everything; we just need to wait out the night. Brij and Rayna dealing with this thing. Have some faith in them; we are here to protect you, Aunty Asha and Maleah. But umm, you need James to see bout that wound 'cause if the infection spread, yuh tolie go rotten and fall off," Alister calmly explained.

Curtis' eyes widened. "Take it! Take off the whole hand, everything," he shrieked in a panic.

James and Alister tried their hardest not to laugh. James knew Alister only added that last bit to get Curtis to cooperate. Grinning slightly, James and Alister made eye contact. James subtly shook his head in disappointment at Alister for playing that prank on Curtis.

Asha stepped out of the room; leaning over slightly, she used her hands to prop on the door frame.

"Asha! Babe, yuh ok? Why yuh out the bed?" asked Curtis worriedly.

Asha took a step forward and stumbled. Curtis flew off the chair and reached out to hold her while Alister grabbed at her. Curtis reached her first and caught her in his arms; Alister held on to them and ensured they were stabilized.

Alister smelled smoke, like burning meat and rotten eggs. He looked down at Curtis' bloody hand, gently touching Asha's arm and smoking at the point of impact.

"What?—" Alister muttered.

Asha let out a scream and backed away from Curtis. "Wah happen?" asked Curtis, confused.

Alister held on to her and inspected the smoking wound on her hand. Her skin was as cold as ice, and the wound appeared to be burnt into it. Alister looked back at Curtis' palm, filled with shards of rusty iron. *It burns because of the iron? How? Unless...* "Curtis, that's not Aunty Asha!" Alister yelled, immediately releasing her as he tried to pull Curtis away.

Possessed by the Churile, Asha's eyes turned white, and her skin began to take on a blueish hue. She grabbed Curtis and tossed him clear across the room like he was weightless, causing him to crash through the kitchen cabinets.

"Exorcizamus Te, Omnis immundus spiritus—" Alister began chanting before he, too, was suddenly thrown backward, crashing through the door and tumbling onto the street. James reached for the hammer, but Asha turned to him with an extended arm. James felt pressure pinning him to the floor, rendering him immobile.

"Omnis Satanica potestas, omnis incursio infernalis adversarii!" Alister shouted from the street. When Asha's eyes returned to normal for a moment, the force keeping James tied down disappeared, so he reached for the hammer again.

"James, no! She's pregnant! Don't hurt her! Just keep her from moving!" Alister yelled out.

Asha's eyes suddenly turned white again, and she screamed, waking the entire village. At the sound of her blood-curdling scream, the villagers peeked through their windows, trying to catch a glimpse of what had made that sound. The streetlights began flickering and dimming the lights in the village. Asha grabbed the iron pipe, and despite her hand sizzling, she raised it high and was about to impale her stomach.

James dashed over, grabbed the hammer, and swung at the pipe to knock it out of Asha's hands. The pipe fell from her grasp, raining down rusty pieces of iron that fell to the floor.

Asha turned to James and walked forward to grab him. But stepping on the rusty iron shards on the ground caused her to scream out in pain and back away.

Alister got to his feet and continued chanting, "Omnis legio, omnis congregatio, et secta diabolica...." He was suddenly yanked off his feet and tossed into the rental car's windshield. His vision blurred as he barely clung to consciousness. The glass on the vehicle began to freeze up like it did with the stove earlier.

A shadowy figure appeared in front of Alister. At that moment, a shotgun went off, and the figure disappeared into thin smoke.

Brij walked into the house quickly, chanting, "Ergo draco maledicte, ecclesiam tuam secure tibi." He splashed Holy Water onto Asha, and her face began to burn and turn reddish. She screamed and jerked about while writhing in pain. Curtis ran to Asha and held her hands down, keeping them away from her

183

belly. "Facias libertate sevire, te rogamus! Audi nos!" Brij finished the chant, poured Holy Water into his hand, and covered Asha's mouth as she screamed; the streetlight in the immediate vicinity blew. She instantly settled down but blacked out. Her skin smoked, and the burning stopped. Her skin regained its natural dark caramel-brown complexion; Brij and Curtis gently placed her on the sofa.

"Asha! Asha! Babe?" Curtis panicked.

"She ok, doh worry. She go just be tired for a lil bit," Brij calmly explained.

"Mr. Curtis, come let me see about your hand, please," said James. Curtis cooperated. He sat down and allowed James to clean his wounds. Alister was brought inside on Rayna's shoulders and placed on the chair beside Asha.

James looked worried at Alister as he lay unconscious. "He alright?" asked James while bandaging Curtis' hand.

"He fine," Rayna sternly replied.

Brij took Curtis' hand and chanted the same incantation they had used to exorcise the Churile from Asha's body.

The blackened mark on Curtis' hand disappeared, and Brij turned to James furiously, not speaking a word.

"Oh gosh, it gone! Meh tolie wouldn't fall out now. Oh, thank God!" Curtis sighed in relief.

Brij and Rayna turned to him in confusion, then quickly diverted their attention to James, who shrugged his shoulders and grinned.

CHAPTER

19

Rayna went into Maleah's room and ensured the Churile didn't attempt to possess her. Brij watched Alister and Asha on the chair while Curtis paced the room. James stood in a corner with his eyes glued to Alister.

"I thought I tell ulyuh this life is not for y'all. Look around! This man and he wife in bad shape, and yuh jackass cousin almost dead. What woulda happen if we wasn't here? Ulyuh head so hard, boy? Losing Raphael and them lil children wasn't enough? Yuh had to come here and put these people and yuhself in danger again?" Brij scoffed in a harsh tone.

"Why you doh hull yuh mudda cunt…," James retorted.

"Buh A A. What is that?" asked Curtis.

"Excuse?" Brij replied simultaneously.

"Fuck you, Brij. You hit the nail on the head when you tell my cousin the Trini in he does come out when he vex. Yeah, I didn't grow up here like him, but I am still a Trini, and I'm tired of you. If we weren't here, Asha would have still been possessed. The Churile could have killed her unborn child and maybe the rest of them along with it. So, where were you, Mr. Hunter?" James snapped.

"She pregnant?" Brij asked, concerned. Rayna peeked from the doorway at the sound of the commotion.

"Yeah, she's pregnant. What? With all of your hunter experience, you couldn't figure that out?" James shot back.

Brij turned to Curtis, "You didn't tell meh she was pregnant."

"Buh widdi jail, how dais your business? A man barge into your house, and the first thing yuh go tell him is yuh wife pregnant just so? Yuh never ask. How I go know that had anything to do with anything," Curtis replied.

"Alister knew since yesterday. That's why he came back here because of what he knew a day in advance, and your old ass was too stubborn to listen. They are alive because of us; no, no... They are alive because of Alister. Yeah, we almost got them killed in the process, but whose fault is that? You refused to train us, and you left them unguarded. We cleaned up your mess, and you want to talk about my cousin and me like that? You fucking piece of—" James uttered before he was cut off.

"Enough," Alister mumbled; he leaned forward in the chair and held the back of his head. "It's been a while since I heard you curse like a Trini," Alister chuckled.

"You alright?" James quickly asked.

"Yeah, I'll live," Alister replied. "Look, no point in going at each other's throats now; we have plenty of time for that when we finish this job. Like it or not, we are all here and share a similar goal."

"If two ah ulyuh didn't come and move the shoes, the Churile woulda still be trapped," Brij retorted.

"The shoes?" James exclaimed in confusion.

"I doh have time to explain to you in detail. But the shoes we leave on the road woulda keep the Churile in one place for the duration of the night and give we time to find the body. And by blessing the bones, we'd let the spirit of that woman pass on to the other side," Brij quickly explained.

"Yeah, we know if you leave a pair of shoes behind, the Churile will spend the night trying to put it on," James remarked. Rayna was stunned; Brij looked at James in shock. "And we didn't see any shoes," James continued.

"By chance, was it an old pair of sneakers?" Alister asked curiously.

"Yeah…," Brij slowly replied.

"Walk outside and look up on the streetlamp. Tell me if that is the same pair. When we pulled up, it was still swinging like somebody threw it up there," Alister informed them.

Like Alister suggested, Brij, Alister, and James walked into the street and looked up to find the pair of shoes tangled on the streetlight.

"How the ass it reach dey? That not possible! A Churile couldn't put on the shoes, much less throw them up a streetlight," Brij exclaimed

"Brij, if yuh exorcize the Churile from Asha, what was outside to throw Alister on the car? 'Cause I shot at something," said Rayna from the door.

"Is more than one… Churiles can't cross water, so something else killed the vagrant on the other side of the river," Alister surmised.

"Fuck—" Brij mumbled.

Rayna was suddenly tossed back inside from the doorway. The door slammed shut, and the house's windows began to frost up. The remaining lights inside the house and the street flickered. Rayna was lifted off the ground and suspended in the air a few feet off the floor. The spirit of the Churile's husband appeared, holding Rayna by the throat.

"The Fish Man!" Curtis exclaimed, recognizing the person.

Rayna was tossed across the room; she used the momentum and angled her body so that her feet would make contact with the wall first. With both feet planted against the wall, Rayna quickly drew the gun from her jacket and fired at the ghost of the Fisherman. He vanished into smoke just as Brij and the boys came crashing through the door. Rayna fell to the ground but landed on her feet.

"Rayna!" Brij cried out.

"Brij, it was the fisherman... The lady who husband get bounce," Rayna notified him.

"How come? What keeping him here? They does burn bodies at funerals in Trinidad, so he ghost shouldn't be roaming," Brij remarked.

"You want to fill us in?" asked Alister.

"No!" answered Rayna and Brij in unison.

"They talking about the couple who died here a while back. That man and he wife was in a hit-and-run. They say he wife had an outside man, but the outside man didn't know she was married, and when he find out, he run them over with he car," Curtis explained.

"Ever occur to you that the husband also didn't know she had ah outside man? Maybe he can't rest 'cause of his wife. As long as she roaming, he might be roaming too!" Alister proposed.

Brij and Rayna looked at each other in shock. "He has a point, inno," Rayna muttered.

"Fuck… Alright, fine. Listen up, we need to find the body of the woman and bless the bones so she will pass on to the afterlife; burning it will do the same thing. Our priority is finding those bones, all of it," Brij announced to the group.

"Where are these bones?" asked James.

"The river. The police report says the body most likely fell into the river; since it runs from the mountain into the village, we can narrow it down," Brij answered.

"Wait, yuh mean the river that runs through the back of the house? Yuh know how far that river does go? It does take two hours to hike to the top, and then it does lead down to the pools. That could take a day alone to look, plus ulyuh hada do that in the night? Who go stay here and protect we?" asked Curtis worriedly.

"How long ago was this? I mean, it's a river; it constantly changes because it's always flowing. Those bones could be covered beneath the dirt and mud at the bottom. We would never know?" James exclaimed.

"Oh yes, we would!" Rayna said as she reached into her jacket and pulled out a device. "This is an EMF reader; once we close enough, we will get the reading on this. Then we just dig till we find it."

"Ok, sounds like a plan to me," Alister agreed.

"Curtis, you still have that walkie-talkie, right?" asked Brij.

"Yeah, it in the room," Curtis replied.

"Ok, Alister, you take this," Brij gave Alister an EMF reader. "Keep this on; when you get readings, it means ghosts are around. We not just dealing with a Churile here. Curtis, yuh have salt? Plenty salt?"

"I have a five-pound bag, yeah," Curtis responded.

"Ok, you, Alister, listen carefully. By the windows and doors, draw a line with salt in front of them. No ghost would be able to enter. The Churile, however, is a next story. Take this," Brij said as he handed Alister his handgun and the extra magazines of iron rounds. "This will repel the Churile. Don't waste your bullets on the Fisherman ghost, yuh hear meh?" Brij warned.

"Yeah, understood," Alister replied.

"When we find the bones and burn it, we gonna call you on this and let you know the coast clear," Brij continued.

"No problem," said Alister.

"James, you coming with we. We need more eyes looking because we only have one EMF now," said Brij.

"Alright," James answered.

"Rayna, give him your shotgun," Brij instructed. "Ok, lewe get this done. Soon as we leave, salt them doors and windows. Doh worry about Asha being possessed again. The Holy Water in she system so she would be spirit free till it pass from she body. Just tell she to try not to pee," Brij remarked.

Alister walked up to James while Rayna quickly showed him how to operate the shotgun. "Be safe out there, bro," Alister told him as he and James bumped fists.

"What about me?" asked Rayna.

"I'll pray for the ghost," Alister replied as he turned, walked back inside, and followed Brij's instructions.

CHAPTER

20

Brij, Rayna, and James headed back to the river with the EMF in hand while Alister and Curtis salted the doors and windows of the house. They kept a keen eye on the EMF reader Brij had left with them. Curtis walked up to Alister after they completed their task and asked, "How yuh know we was in danger? Why yuh come back?"

"Remember when we took the family picture?" Alister replied as he took his phone out of his pocket. He found the picture he was referring to and showed it to Curtis. "Look at Aunty Asha's face. Her eyes white here. At first, I thought it was just a lens flare. But then I learned about this thing that haunting the village, and it started to line up with the stuff you told me about what was happening. I started getting a bad feeling, and I just needed to come make sure you, the child, and Aunty Asha were safe," Alister explained.

"Who teach ulyuh about these things? Yuh mother know yuh does do this?" asked Curtis curiously.

"No, and please don't mention this to her if we manage to live. This isn't the first time I have been in this situation, but that one ended badly. My aunt married a guy named Raphael; he was like a father figure to all of us. Even though he had no kids, he treated us like we were his own. He wanted to protect us from all of this, but things got dark really fast, and we had no choice but to learn how to do this. He died saving us, but he left his legacy for me to continue because he saw something in me," Alister answered. "To be honest, I wish he didn't, but when I think about how much evil is really out there and how he gave his life for us, I thought, 'What kind of person would turn their back on so many people who needed someone to save them.' You know?"

"Look at you, nah. I remember you as a small lil boy, always excited to come Maracas for the weekend. You were always running ahead ah we and going in the water early morning. But yuh all grown up now," Curtis reminisced.

"I don't feel grown up; I make so many mistakes it's like I'm still the little boy you remember," Alister mumbled.

"Being grown up doh mean yuh perfect. Mistakes happen, and yuh go make a lot of them. But life is about learning from your mistakes. Look how yuh pelt meh with the hammer; I sure next time yuh would practice aiming before yuh hit somebody again," Curtis chuckled. Alister grinned and looked at him.

"Sorry about that, by the way," said Alister.

"Daz nothing. Dah go heal, and ah go learn from it. Next time, I'll know to move when you pelting," Curtis chuckled. "But dais how life is; it will hurt now, and mistakes will happen, but it wouldn't hurt forever. And next time, yuh wouldn't repeat the same mistakes. Yuh save Asha, and yuh save the child she pregnant with. No words will ever be able to tell you how much I am grateful for you. Doh worry, yuh secret safe with we. Moms wouldn't find out from us."

The two sat silently for a few minutes before the EMF reader started going wild. The windows began to frost up; Curtis went next to Asha and held her in his arms. "The Fishman come back," Curtis remarked.

"I hope that salt line would stop the Churile," Alister muttered as he drew the gun.

"Bredda… Bredda, I go take a hammer but make sure yuh aim properly with that gun. God give me enough holes," Curtis cried out worriedly.

Alister looked around with the gun in hand; he turned to see the Churile exiting the bedroom. It turned to him, its white eyes glaring at him. Alister squeezed the trigger, but it didn't budge.

"The safety still on!" Curtis called out. Alister inspected the gun for the safety lock. By the time he'd unlocked it and looked up, the Churile was beside him, grabbing hold of him and tossing him into the wall, the gun falling out of his hand.

The Churile's screech woke Asha; Curtis held on to her tight as she screamed at the sight of the creature, and he quickly covered her mouth. The Churile vanished and appeared at the foot of Alister; still on the floor, Curtis grabbed the hammer and threw it at the Churile.

Missing, the hammer hit the wooden kitchen cabinet behind and got wedged into it.

The Churile turned to Curtis and screamed. Holding its hand out, Curtis was sent flying back into the chair. The sheer force of the impact sent the couch dragging across the room and into the wall. Alister got to his feet, pried the hammer from the cabinet, and swung through at the Churile's body, making it vanish into thin smoke.

"Not so easy to aim a hammer, ent?" Alister called out, still partially winded from being tossed into the wall.

"Bredda, I know I miss the jumbie, but at least I didn't hit yuh. Ease meh up," Curtis responded with his breathing out of control.

"Alister? Oh gosh, yuh ok," asked Asha.

"Of course. If Curtis didn't save all ah we just now, we woulda be dead," Alister answered as he winked at Curtis.

"Curtis?? Save we?? Nah!" Asha replied, shaking her head.

"Oh gosh, yuh doh have to say it so," Curtis retorted.

"Is true. Watch how he hand and leg get. He fighting jumbie whole night," Alister informed her.

"Jumbie? Ulyuh serious? Is really ah jumbie?" Asha questioned.

"I wish I coulda tell yuh no, but dais the shit we in right now. Yuh get possessed earlier, and it almost killed the child," Alister explained.

"Oh gosh, Maleah… She ok?" asked Asha, panicked.

"Not that one," Alister answered as he pointed at her belly.

"Oh shux…," Asha gasped.

"Again, if Curtis didn't save yuh and fight off that jumbie by heself—" Alister began before he was cut off.

"Nah, nah, nah, nope. Dais enough. Me eh wah she thinking I is some hero before she start sending me to fight people. I good, bredda.

Alister and he cousin do all the fighting," Curtis frantically corrected.

"Ah shock!" Asha teased sarcastically and rolled her eyes.

"Doh worry, we should be ok. Brij and them working on it now; we just need to wait it out," Alister informed her.

"What if it come back and possess me again?" Asha enquired.

"You go be ok. Brij say don't pee. As long as the Holy Water is in your system, you go be ghost-free," Alister replied.

"What about the rest ah ulyuh? Ulyuh drink Holy Water too?" asked Asha.

"Nah," said Curtis.

"So you mean Maleah could get possessed, too?" Asha exclaimed.

"Doh worry, Alister go make sure the jumbie don't get near we. He have a device that does tell yuh when it close, so once it goes off, he go hit it with some iron and we good till it come back," answered Curtis.

"Actually, she has a point. I mean, the smart thing to do woulda be to give everybody some Holy Water to drink. That way, we wouldna be at risk of being possessed," Alister remarked.

"Yuh have any more?" asked Curtis.

"Nah, it wasn't mine; Brij is the one who had," Alister replied. "But I bet we could make some."

***

Brij, Rayna, and James were walking quickly along the riverbank when Alister called in on the walkie-talkie. "Brij, can you hear me?" asked Alister.

Brij took the walkie-talkie off his belt and held it to his mouth. "Yeah, wah happen?" Brij replied.

"How possible is it to make Holy Water? Like anybody could do it, or do we need a priest like in the movies," Alister enquired.

"Why you need Holy Water? Ent yuh salt the doors and windows? No ghost could come inside," Brij responded.

"We did, but it couldn't keep the Churile out. It already attacked once since then," Alister informed him.

"Use the gun, nah, jackass," Brij snapped.

"I did, but we uneasy here; the Churile could possess somebody else," said Alister.

"The lady have Holy Water in her system; she go be ok. Churiles doh possess men," answered Brij.

"I'm aware, but it still have a girl child in the house; it would be a little comforting to give her some, too," Alister replied.

"Brij, just tell him how to do it if you know," James commented.

"Shut yuh ass and keep looking. Nobody talking to you," Brij snapped. He held the walkie-talkie to his mouth again. "Listen, I didn't give yuh the walkie-talkie to waste time like this; I give yuh a gun and the know-how to fend off ghosts. Stop asking dotish questions and keep that family safe."

***

Alister put down the walkie-talkie after Brij ended the conversation. "Buh he rude! Somebody go slap down he old ass one ah these days," Asha stated.

"I tempted…," said Alister as he sat down and took out his phone. He softly whispered to himself, "What is Latin for Holy Water?"

CHAPTER

21

Along the bank of the river, the EMF reader started getting a solid reading; Rayna swept the device and pinpointed the location of the readings. Brij turned his high-powered flashlight to the water and found a piece of clothing wiggling at the bottom of the riverbed.

"Jump in," Rayna told James.

"What? Why me?" asked James.

Rayna pushed James into the shallow river. Falling to his hands and knees, he splashed in the water.

"Pull the body out; we need to bless the bones. Can't burn it 'cause of the water and gas expensive," said Brij.

"How am I going to find all the bones?" questioned James.

"Relax, bodies does decompose slower underwater. Ent you is a Med student? You should know that," Rayna replied.

"How you know that? I never told you I did Med," James exclaimed.

"Raphael talked about 'his boys' a lot. We know all about the October family," Rayna answered.

"Hurry yuh ass up and get the body nah, before the Churile come here," Brij called out.

James used his hands and dug until he found the body, thankfully still intact; he carefully lifted the corpse out of the water, primarily bones and raggedy clothing.

Brij sprinkled the body with salt and Holy Water and began chanting, "Exorcizamus te, omnis—"

Rayna helped James out of the water while Brij recited the incantation. "Yuh alright?" asked Rayna with a smile.

"I gonna be sick, but I'm ok," James responded.

"Doh be a baby; yuh doing Med, yuh should be comfortable around these things," said Rayna.

"Usually, these things are living when I have to be around them," James replied.

"Te rogamus, audi nos!" Brij ended. The corpse began to smoke white.

"What's happening?" asked James.

"Smoke means it worked; the remainder of the soul trapped here finally passed on," Rayna explained.

Brij got the walkie-talkie and called Alister.

***

"Yuh dey boy?" said Brij.

Alister picked up the walkie-talkie, "Yeah, I'm here," he answered.

"We find the body. We gonna be heading back now," Brij informed him. "Organise yuhself, we go give ulyuh a tow back home. Yuh go cyah drive with that windshield so."

"Alright, no problem," Alister answered. He ended the call and smiled. Looking up at Curtis and Asha, he notified them of the good news. "They get through. Ulyuh go be safe now."

"Thank God, yes. So Maleah go be ok?" Asha asked.

"Yeah, she will be; once they kill the thing that did this to her, the effects will go away. She would be ok," Alister comforted. "Guess I wouldn't need this again," he mumbled as he looked at the translation of a page from the book he'd made a digital copy of from Raphael's library.

"What ulyuh gonna do now?" asked Curtis.

"They on their way back; soon as they reach, we will get a lift home," Alister replied.

"Oh gosh, I could finally go pee," Asha said, relieved, as she got up and hurried to the washroom.

"What about the Fishman? They kill he too?" Curtis enquired.

"He should be gone too, now that he wife finally passed on," Alister explained.

"That was horrible, boy. And how Asha get possessed, I doh know how I going to sleep now inno. That go be burned into my memory forever," said Curtis.

"You can't live in fear; I know this is traumatizing, but know it have people out there like Brij and Rayna who hunting these things to keep people safe," Alister consoled him.

"I wish he had give we some of that Holy Water so I could give them every day, yes," said Curtis.

"Well, I know how to do it now; you want me to try and make it for you?" asked Alister.

"Ent yuh need a priest to do them thing?" Curtis exclaimed.

"This is a much older way than how they do it now; the instructions didn't say you needed a priest or anything. Just two ingredients and the right incantation. I have it here if you want to try it," Alister informed him.

"Why not? I go take anything, yes," Curtis affirmed.

"Ok, we just need some water and a lil bit of salt," Alister remarked.

Curtis gathered the two ingredients for Alister. "I need one more thing; by chance, you have a rosary?" Alister asked.

"Nah, boy, we don't have any," Curtis answered.

"Well, I don't need it, but it say you need a blessed object to finalize the process. I think I have a workaround. I know how to bless and

213

purify anything," said Alister. "Oh wait, I already have a blessed object; I could just use that." Alister got the charm from around his neck.

"Aye aye, what kind of devil thing is that you have on yuh neck?" Curtis questioned upon seeing the necklace.

"You mean the star? No, no, no, that is not devil thing. Is actually the opposite. The pentagram is a symbol of protection to keep you safe from evil," Alister explained.

"Or hor," said Curtis.

"Ok, I have the stuff; time to try this," Alister said.

"How you go know if it work? I mean, what if you do it and nothing happen?" asked Curtis.

"The book says it will smoke for a moment; that's when the impurities would leave the water," Alister answered.

"Ok, ok, well go ahead then," said Curtis.

Alister began to recite the incantation Raphael had taught them. As he came to a close, he recited an extra incantation needed for the ritual, "Te rogamus, audi nos. In nomine Patris et Filii et Spiritus Sancti." Alister sprinkled a pinch of salt into the water and broke the water's surface with the key to Raphael's library. The water's surface released a thin layer of white smoke and quickly dissipated into the air.

"Aye, aye, aye, watch how it smoke up. Yuh wuking man!" Curtis cheered, high-fiving Alister. "Way, Asha? She taking too long to pee, boy." Curtis walked off in the direction of the washroom and knocked on the door.

Alister put the charm back around his neck, tucking it under his shirt, so it stayed hidden. Suddenly, the EMF started going off again. Alister looked at it and quickly picked it up. "The fisherman? I guess he didn't pass on with his wife," Alister muttered. Alister turned, and the readings grew stronger in the direction of Curtis.

"Babe?" Curtis called out.

"Curtis, get the door open now!" Alister shouted as he rushed to them and grabbed the Holy Water. Curtis got the spare key off the wall and unlocked the door. A loud crash flung the door open and sent Curtis crashing into Alister. Asha stepped out of the washroom, her skin taking on a blue hue and her eyes white again.

Curtis and Alister scurried off the floor. "I thought they say it gone?" Curtis worriedly asked.

"I thought so, too," Alister replied. "How did they get the Churile out of her before? Did the chant I was saying work?" he asked Curtis.

"Ammm, I doh know. How the ass yuh want me know?" asked Curtis.

"Just think, how did it stop before?" Alister calmly asked.

"Ammm, Brij throw Holy Water in she mouth," Curtis recalled.

"Alright! Hold she down!" Alister instructed as he and Curtis rushed toward Asha. Asha's scream could be heard from the river where Brij and the others were.

***

"The hell?" Brij remarked as he quickly grabbed the walkie-talkie and called Alister.

***

"Alister!... Alister!" Brij's voice came through the walkie-talkie.

Curtis tried to hold Asha down while Alister poured Holy Water into her mouth. The skin around her mouth and throat burned and smoked. Asha grabbed Curtis and flung him into the wall.

"Widdi ass… It stop she immediately last time—" Curtis remarked holding his chest. Asha choked Curtis and lifted him from the floor. Alister rushed in to help, but she swung Curtis like a ragdoll, hitting Alister with his

217

body. The bottle of Holy Water flew out of his grasp and spilled onto the floor. Alister quickly saw this and rushed for the bottle.

With Asha's hand on his neck, a reddish black mark began to spread rapidly over Curtis' body. "Curtis!" Alister screamed. Alister kicked Holy Water up from the puddle, sprinkling some on Asha and Curtis. As the droplets burned her, she released her hold on Curtis.

"Why the hell it not working... Think.... Think.... Fuck, I have no choice," Alister drew the gun and aimed at Asha's shoulder.

"Wait...Wai..." Curtis shouted before he began to feel weak, his consciousness fading. "Before... The water... He was saying...," Curtis mumbled before he blacked out and fell to the ground.

"What!? What was he saying," Alister panicked. Hesitantly, he contemplated pulling the trigger since he knew the iron rounds would repel the Churile from her body. But he would ultimately wound Asha badly in the process.

Alister remembered the moment the gun fired off when Rayna and Brij first arrived. He was losing consciousness after being thrown through the car's windshield, but the loud sound of the shotgun alerted him for a moment. That's when he recalled Brij chanting, "Ergo draco maledicte—"

"Son of a bitch, he was continuing the purification incantation," Alister muttered. Lowering the gun, he began chanting loudly; each word he said seemed to cause the Churile more and more pain inside Asha's body. He approached the end of the incantation. Alister grasped the bottle with barely a mouthful left and grabbed Asha. As she screamed, he poured the water into her mouth. Her skin began to smoke, and the Churile's spirit could be seen flying out of her body, disappearing into thin smoke. Asha fainted in his arms; Alister held her up and quickly took her to the chair, returning shortly after for Curtis.

He ran to his side and sat beside him, reciting the incantation one more time. He placed his hand on Curtis and purified the evil touch of the Churile from his body. Still blacked out, Alister dragged him to the chair and kept him close to Asha. The walkie-talkie came on again. "Alister! Yuh there, boy?!" Brij repeated.

Alister grabbed the walkie-talkie and answered furiously, "I thought you said you finished it!"

"We purified the bones, I'm sure of it. I don't know how it's still roaming; listen, get that family and take my truck. Get them as far from here as you can," Brij replied.

"And what about the rest of the village?" Alister questioned.

"We can't save everybody; nobody will even leave dey house. We doh even have transport for the whole village," Brij responded.

"Brij, yuh can't just pick who you save and leave the rest. We need to do something. We need to figure out why it is still here and kill it before it returns. I almost had to shoot Aunty Asha to get the Churile out," said Alister.

"What?—" Brij uttered.

"Brij... We have a problem," Rayna called out as she and James lifted multiple bones from the river.

"Oh fuck...," Brij exclaimed.

"What! What happening? Brij talk to meh!" Alister yelled.

"Alister, it get a little more complicated; it have more than one body in the river. They just find two different sets of bones, and the body too far gone, so it is not intact. Them bones could be anywhere," Brij explained. James and Rayna pulled up two more bodies.

"These are still bloated; this couldn't be more than a day or two old," James informed them.

"It's dumping the victims in the river—" Rayna exclaimed.

"Which means any one of them could be the Churile's human corpse... Fuck!" said Brij.

"Then keep blessing them until you find the right one," Alister remarked.

"You doh understand; it's not that simple. The bones that scattered could take days to find. We need to get the police to come and drag the entire river to make sure we get every last bone; if we miss even one, the Churile will remain anchored here," Brij explained.

James suddenly got yanked off his feet and flung into the bushes. Rayna quickly drew her gun and fired at the spirit of the Fisherman who appeared. "James!" Rayna called out as she ran into the bushes to get him.

"What… What happened to James!" Alister asked worriedly as he heard the commotion in the background.

"He get attacked by the Fisherman; listen to me, get that family out of here now. That woman is pregnant. I cannot afford to worry about the entire village, but at the very least, save them. Get them out of the village and pass the bridge when you leave Maracas. Come back as soon as you can and help we keep the Churile at bay. We have enough bullets to hold it off for the night," said Brij.

"With Aunty Asha out of the village, the Churile will not have a set target. It's coming after her because she is pregnant; if we take her away, then it would torment the rest of the village. We must have some other option here, Brij," Alister remarked. Curtis slowly opened his eyes as he regained consciousness.

"Listen!!! I tell yuh that yuh cannot let emotions cloud yuh judgment. So what if the rest of the village get attacked? Yuh prefer that family get killed instead? Because when it kill she family, it still going to torment the village and the outsiders that come here. This is how it does work. People does dead, and yuh cyah save everybody! Now get them out of here, or you get yuh ass up here and help we keep the Churile from killing anybody else in the village because we can't purify all these bodies. We would never find them all under the water!" Brij retorted.

The Holy Water that spilled from the bottle flowed to the door and broke the salt line. The sound of the windows icing up diverted Alister's attention as the Fisherman appeared in the room. Alister quickly drew the gun and fired, repelling the ghost. "Alister! Alister, yuh hear meh, boy?!" said Brij through the walkie-talkie.

Alister looked at the walkie-talkie in his hand. *So, they can't purify all the bodies underwater...* he thought. "Holy shit... I got it!" Alister muttered as he ran to the kitchen.

He grabbed the bag of salt and took out a handful. Giving Curtis the bag, he instructed, "Salt back the door when I leave."

"LEAVE?!" Curtis all but yelled.

"Trust me," Alister said as he opened the door, ran out, and headed to the river.

***

"Alister!!! This jackass!" Brij grumbled.

"What happened?" asked Rayna and James, coming back from the bushes.

"Alister not answering," Brij replied.

***

Alister sprinted and lept into the water. "Churiles can't cross water; I should be safe here," he said. Alister drew the gun in case the Fisherman's ghost showed up again. "Please work…. Here goes nothing."

Alister looked around, took a deep breath, and took the charm off his neck. "Exorcizamus te!..." Alister began chanting.

EXORCIZAMUS TE

***

"Omnis immundus spiritus!" Alister continued. Brij, Rayna, and James heard Alister in the distance.

The trio turned to the sound of his voice projecting in the distance as he repeated the incantation.

"What the hell he trying to do?" asked Brij.

"Is he trying to exorcise the Churile?" James wondered.

Rayna grabbed James and pulled him behind her as she ran toward Alister.

***

"Ergo Draco Maledicte!" Alister chanted. The Churile and the ghost of the Fisherman appeared on both sides of the riverbank. "Ecclesiam tuam secri tibi facias!" he continued, firing at the fisherman and then the Churile. Both kept reappearing moments after being shot. Alister soon emptied the clip and needed to change the magazine but couldn't.

The Fisherman pulled Alister from the water and tossed him onto the ground. He threw some salt at the ghost, repelled it for a moment, and tried to run back to the water. But his efforts were in vain. He soon found himself being dragged off the ground again and pinned to a coconut tree.

"Hey!" Rayna shouted as they ran toward him. She tossed the shotgun to James and drew her handgun. "Don't shoot; you could hit him from this far!" she told James as she fired the bullet. The Churile vanished into smoke again. The force pinning Alister to the tree had disappeared, and he fell to the ground. Appearing before him again was the Fisherman; James raised the gun just beside the head of the Fisherman and fired. Extending his hand, he pulled Alister to his feet.

"Hold them off!" said Alister, running back and jumping into the river.

"What the hell are you doing?" asked Rayna with her gun aimed and looking around.

"Libertate servire, te rogamus!" Alister chanted.

"The hell is he doing?" Rayna whispered.

"Audi nos. In nomine Patris et Filii et Spiritus Sancti!!!" Alister pulled the charm from his neck with the hand filled with salt. He slammed his hand into the water, grasping Raphael's charm tightly.

The water along the river began to smoke. Some places even began shooting smoke into the air like a geyser.

Brij came running down the bank in time to see Alister do this; he turned and watched as the water's surface expelled smoke, covering the village in a thin fog for a moment. The screams of the Churile and the Fisherman faded into the air. They appeared along the river and burned away into the fog.

"Well, I'll be… He blessed the water in

the river—" Brij exclaimed. He slowly turned to see Alister standing up from the water, holding Raphael's key tight in his palm. Alister looked at Brij with piercing eyes, knowing he had spotted Raphael's key.

CHAPTER

22

Eyes locked, Brij reached into his pocket and retrieved the protection charm he had taken from Alister. Brij aimed his gun at Alister, "Yuh sneaky lil bitch. This one is ah fake, ent?!"

"Brij?" said Rayna.

Alister tightened his grip on Raphael's real protection charm. Brij glared at him as he aimed the gun at his head from the riverbank.

"Brij!" Rayna screamed.

The sound of a shotgun racking turned their attention toward Rayna; James had put the barrel of the gun to her head. "Drop it! Or I will drop her!" James fiercely remarked. "Stay still, Rayna. You even tremble, and I will shoot. I'll kill you, then Brij'll kill us, and he will spend what little time of his life is left alone. Try me, and find out if I am not willing to die to live up to my words," James finished.

"We just saved this village, Brij; now that the death omen is gone, you are one step closer to finding the harbinger and destroying it," said Alister.

Rayna and Brij's eyes widened as they turned to Alister in surprise.

"You want the horsemen? How about two extra hands purging this world of the harbingers? All I want is the right to hunt Krampus; Quattuor Equites is yours. But we can't kill Krampus as we are now, and I am no longer asking for your permission. So shoot me if you want to stop us, or you can stop being stuck in your old ways and teach us," Alister continued.

Brij's hand holding the gun shook. Alister calmly walked from the water and onto the riverbank. He marched up to Brij and placed his forehead on the gun's barrel. "This only ends one way, Brij. You will end up alone, no matter how this goes down. We either die trying to vanquish the evil from this earth or right here at your hand. I was born here; there isn't a place in the world I would rather die," Alister exclaimed.

Brij looked past Alister to Rayna with the gun to her head. Alister grabbed the gun and pushed it away from his head, followed by a crushing right hook. Brij's feet left the ground for a split second; the force of Alister's punch threw him to the floor. Alister broke Brij's grip on his gun and stole it from his grasp the moment he'd hit him. He then quickly aimed the gun at Brij on the floor.

"Brij!!!" Rayna yelled out, worried.

Alister mercilessly pulled the trigger as Brij looked up at him from the ground. Firing twice, the gun clicked, but no shots left the gun's barrel. Rayna gasped.

"Boom! And you're dead," Alister declared as he raised his hand and showed Brij he had removed the magazine before he fired, tossing it at his feet. Alister extended his hand to Brij; he grabbed hold of it and was pulled to his feet.

Dusting himself off, Brij chuckled. "Now that is how yuh supposed to hit," Brij remarked. James lowered his gun and gave it to Rayna, tapping her on the shoulder as he walked past her and over to Alister.

Alister and James bumped fists. "That was sick, man," said James. "How did you know how to do that?"

"I learned from the instructions that making Holy Water was simple enough. It said nothing about a max capacity, so I figured it might work," Alister explained.

"No, no, not that. I mean, how did you pull the magazine from the gun that fast? We don't have any shooting experience, and we could barely use a hammer to fight earlier without hurting Curtis," James chuckled.

"A hammer? Why?" asked Rayna.

"Well, we don't exactly have an arsenal like you guys, so we had to improvise. Hammers are made from pure iron mostly, and it's a household object you can find in almost every home. That was our best bet to repel the Churile if it showed," Alister answered.

"And the gun? How yuh really do that so fast? Actually, how yuh even know to do that at all? Change release a magazine?" asked Brij.

"Well, when the Churile attacked, the safety was on, so I almost got Curtis and them killed when the gun didn't fire. I don't like not knowing about something; I think if you do something, you do it to the best of your ability. So I spent a little time figuring out the gun and did a little research. I fiddled with it enough to see how it works and how to reload," Alister explained.

Brij smiled, "I see... Well, come lewwe get out of here; I want some tea, and I sure Rayna hungry. Ulyuh boys do good today, come I'll tow ulyuh car back."

Alister knocked on the door of Asha's house; Curtis opened the door briefly after. He and Asha were burnt out and just wanted the night to be over. Alister hugged them both and assured them everything was over now and the village and their daughter were safe again. Brij and the group piled into his truck; with no place for all four of them, Alister chose to lie down in the tray. He waved at Asha and Curtis as they drove off, ensuring they were safe now. Alister gazed at the stars on their drive back to Endeavor.

***

Brij stopped at the food strip for the three to get something to eat. Rayna came to the tray and leaned over with her arms folded on the side of the tray. "Wah yuh feeling for?" Rayna asked.

"Food," said Alister with a smirk.

"Yeah, no shit, sherlock," Rayna chuckled and rolled her eyes.

"You like to eat, right? I sure you tasted some good food before. Recommend me something," Alister suggested.

"Gyro?" asked Rayna.

"What's that?" Alister enquired.

"I keep forgetting you leave when you was younger," said Rayna. "Chicken, beef, or lamb?" she asked.

"I never had lamb before. I'll try that one," said Alister.

"Bet," said Rayna, walking off to the food vendors with James accompanying her.

Brij came to the other side of Alister, still lying in the tray. "Yuh ok?" asked Brij.

"For the most part. I still trying to wrap my head around this whole monsters and evil thing," Alister replied.

"Raphael wouldn't be proud, yuh know," said Brij; Alister looked at him confused. "Raphael loved you boys like his own; he didn't have kids because ah we family legacy. It is not easy being born in the Mohan family. Brij senior, my father, was a tyrant. Brilliant man, strong like ah ox, but he was harsh, and he raised his family into this life. I had twelve brothers—" Rayna interrupted Brij and gave him a cup of green tea to drink. "Thanks, Rayna," he said before taking a sip.

Rayna and James climbed into the tray with Alister, handing him his gyro; Alister sat upright in the tray as Brij continued speaking to him. "Twelve boys; by the time I was twenty, it had four left. And before I turned twenty-five, I was the only one remaining," Brij explained. "I was left raising their kids on my own, and my brothers' kids who they left behind. I raised them all into this life; it's a big family. You know how many are left?" asked Brij.

"Six, plus you and Rayna," said Alister confidently.

"Correct is right. The six hunters, plus my great-granddaughter and myself, are all that's left of this family. Boys, Raphael had no kids of his own because this is the fate of those who are born under our lineage; he couldn't handle bringing someone into this life and raising them like this.

"This family is mainly boys; for three generations, all we had was boys, and then this little gem was born, meh first and only great-granddaughter. She think I does be hard on she and too protective, and she damn right! I bury too many people to send more to their deaths, and Raphael would have never wanted this for you boys. He had to be consumed with a vengeance to make that dotish call and leave his legacy for ulyuh to pick up. But I glad he did. Yuh do nothing but surprise me and exceed my expectations of you as a person since you step foot through my door. People doh fool me;

people doh trick me jusso. But one thing that never happen to me is meeting somebody who overshoot my expectations.

"Raphael saw your potential, and the longer I interact with ulyuh, I figuring it out too. Ulyuh is a whole new type of hunter; we family old school, we do things by the book, but you? Yuh creative, yuh resourceful, and yuh resilient. We might be looking at a new generation of hunters, but we might also be looking at the last of them too. We have never been this close to my father's goal, which was to banish evil from the earth forever. I go assume yuh break into the library at some point and read about Quattuor Equites. We this close to ending it. Two hunters each killing off the lines of each of them. We just successfully destroyed the last of the Eques Famis line, and now it gonna draw out the harbinger, a Soucouyant. A bloodthirsty fire demon, the harbinger of Eques Famis.

"What we see today was nothing; this particular harbinger has the second highest death toll, and the famine métier between a harbinger and a descendant of the line is unfathomable. When it shows up, this entire island will be under its effect, not just ah few people in ah tiny village. The closer it is, the stronger its effect; that's how we find it," Brij explained.

"It was a spawn of the line; everything comes from the horsemen. The harbinger creatures spawns, then those spawns create spawns, and so on. Each one weaker than its 'parent,' so to speak," Rayna continued.

"The Churile is the last of the line. It is the Death Omen of the harbinger. All that remains is the harbinger and the Horseman of Famine, so we need to be ready for this fight," Brij declared.

"We?" asked Alister.

Brij nodded his head 'yes' and sipped his tea. "I want you and James hunting the line of

Eques Victoriae. Raphael's legacy was killing that line. The other six hunters are after the remaining three. I'll train ulyuh and teach yuh everything I know. But under one condition…," Brij stated as he turned to Rayna. "You take Rayna with you."

Rayna looked at Brij with shock on her face; Alister and James looked at each other before looking back at Brij. "What?" said James.

"I sheltered her for too long. She begged to be a hunter, and I couldn't bring mehself to let she become one. But I needed somebody with me because of the circumstances and what was at stake today. And in the end, I didn't do anything. You and James pull ulyuh weight, and Alister protected that entire village when I was ready to let them die while trying to kill the Churile the old-fashioned way. Rayna hold she own like a champ today, like a true hunter," Brij smiled. "I'm very proud of you."

Rayna began to tear up. Quickly wiping away the tears, she asked, "You serious?"

"Alister made a good point when I had the gun on him. Everybody will eventually die. I rather ulyuh die fighting for something than being on the sidelines. I will write you a cheque; you should have enough to live comfortably and travel while yuh hunting without any worry for money," Brij remarked.

"Wait, this really happening?" Alister exclaimed.

"Yeah, but I warning you. If you get my grandchild killed, monsters would be the least of your worries 'cause it would have a special place in hell for the things I would do," said Brij sternly.

"Yes sir, understood," Alister extended his hand to Brij and shook his hand.

"Any questions?" asked Brij.

"One but not related to this," said Alister. "If all you do is hunting, how do you have the money to raise so many people and send them all over the world to hunt?"

Brij chuckled as he walked over to the driver's side window. "We have a lil business that does fund everything, plus it does secure weapons and ammo for we. Is how we able to fortify the gates and the structure of the house and even the vehicle with pure iron, so it's safe from most ghosts and creatures."

"What business?" Alister enquired.

"You might remember hearing this as a child before you leave this country," Brij stated. He flipped a switch that prompted two speakers at the top of his truck to rotate from a hidden compartment. The speakers blasted the words Alister and everyone in Trinidad knew, "Buying scrap iron, old battery buying!"

END

Printed in Great Britain
by Amazon

38234522R00145